ACCLAIM FOR PAUL RAMEY'S
EDGAR WILDE AND THE LOST GRIMOIRE!

"From the first page I was completely hooked. . .
you'll find yourself completely immersed in the
beautifully thought-out plot and characters. It
is not often I find a book that feels like an old
friend but this was definitely one."

– BestChapLit.com

"*Edgar Wilde and the Lost Grimoire* was such
a delight to read! Paul Ramey wrote this book
expertly, with the storyline and character de-
velopment perfectly balanced! A definite rec-
ommended read and 5 stars!"

– Old Victorian Quill

". . . a tightly-woven, enthralling novel that will
please readers both young and old. There is
magic here, not only in the grimoire itself, but
in the storytelling. I devoured this novel in two
days, reading through meals and staying up late
into the night with my itty bitty book light. If
that isnt the sign of a great read, I don't know
what is."

– The Pen and Whisk

"Edgar is an engaging hero. . . but the star of the book has to be the beguiling Shelby Emerson, a strong and intelligent female lead that reminded me of Joss Whedon's women – capable, quick and perfectly capable of standing alone while preferring not to. The book, while aimed at young adults, certainly delighted this grumpy old git. Do yourself a favour, give *Edgar Wilde* a couple of hours of your time. You'll be delighted that you did."

– *Cubic Scats*

"It felt like a YA version of a Stephen King or F. Paul Wilson novel. . . Excellent first novel – more!"

– *Project Gemini*

"Starting out with fast-paced intrigue, it doesn't let go of the mystery."

– *Minstrels and Heroes*

"The descriptive prose was beautifully written and the storyline was intriguing and enjoyable. If you like witches, cemeteries, spell books, and mysteries, I recommend this book!"

– *Riverside Reader*

Edgar Wilde and the Lost Grimoire

PAUL RAMEY

NINE MUSE PRESS®

EDGAR WILDE AND THE LOST GRIMOIRE

©2013 by Paul Ramey

All rights reserved.

Cover design by Paul Ramey
Book design by Nine Muse Press

First Printing: April 2013
Nine Muse Press

10 9 8 7 6 5 4 3 2 1

ISBN-978-0-578-12703-3

Find out more about the author and upcoming books
online at www.ninemusepress.com.

Acknowledgments

Eternal gratitude and love to my wife, Tina. Your support, belief, patience, counsel, and incredible work in creating the books web presence are THE reasons this book exists at all. Thanks to my parents, Dan and Betty Ramey. You have never wavered in your support for my many flights of fancy, and I love you so much for it. Brother Greg, you are a constant inspiration and have been a vital sounding board at crucial moments; I thought of you a lot while writing this book.

Thanks to Ingeburg Huggins for the many late nights, staying up with me and watching television while I quietly composed a large part of the first draft of this book. A huge thanks to Susan Colby, who unexpectedly and generously flew us up to Salem, Massachusetts during the writing of this book. Thanks to Daniel Swensen, for taking the time to give my final manuscript the twice-over. Joe Little, youve been a bastion of enthusiasm during the buildup to the release of the book — much gratitude. John Helgren, Martin Raymer and Frances Figart — my journey is your journey, always.

Finally, a deep bow to Anna K. Meade. Your tireless editing of Edgar Wilde and the Lost Grimoire was something akin to alchemy. Enough said.

Edgar Wilde and the Lost Grimoire

Paul Ramey

For Sofia

Chapter 1

April 20, 1724. St. Edmund Island, Massachusetts.

"Here, lass. Rest you easy now. The compound be almost ready."

Goody Wallace glanced over to her patient and forced a comforting smile. In the small bed, 19-year-old Margharet Fullman lay writhing. Strands of blonde hair matted across the young girl's sweat-soaked face as her head turned this way and that, trying to escape the searing flames raging in her belly. Her feeble effort to return the old woman's smile quickly turned to tears.

Goody Wallace squinted at the Grimoire's open pages, double-checking herself before adding a handful of fennel to the boiling paste. The healing poultice was almost complete.

Her fingers moved through the many powders, roots and leaves packed away in her worn cloth pouch until she found the final ingredient. Then, crouching close to the cauldron, she added the required amount of anise powder to the mixture and slowly inhaled the pungent vapors.

"Good," she wiped her tired hands on the corners of her apron, then turned to Margharet. "This will ease the pain and delay the child's arrival. Quickly, it won't survive the heat for long."

Pulling back the sheets, the old woman then scooped some of the hot paste in her hand and smeared it quickly over the girl's swollen belly.

"It's like fire!" the girl contorted. Goody Wallace dabbed a cold compress to her forehead, and waited as the paste began to dry into a map of delicate cracks.

"Breathe deep. Let your flesh take the heat. What burns you for a moment will comfort the little soul inside you. I warrant your child already begins to draw new life."

The old woman wiped her hands clean. After a lifetime of such doctoring she no longer felt the magic's heat. Still, she knew to avoid unnecessary contact. A gift in small quantities became a curse with increased contact. Her dark, leathered hands were evidence enough of that.

Holding the book to her chest in a moment of silent thanks, Goody Wallace then tucked it safely into a special pocket. All that remained was to wash out the cauldron and settle in for the night.

The air was crisp and soothing as she opened the cabin door. After an evening of toiling over a hot cauldron, the icy breeze was a true blessing. Through the trees she could still make out two or three fluttering candles down in the village. It must be well past midnight, she noted as she turned to finish the remaining task. Dragging the cauldron to the door's edge, she carefully tipped it out and watched the remains of the paste drain slowly out onto the grass.

She was just about to lift the cauldron back up when she felt herself freeze in place. A subtle, anxious feeling raced through her abdomen, quickly spreading all through her body. Goody Wallace braced herself — she hadn't felt the *warnings* in years.

Turning first to the girl, then back out into the darkness, the old woman settled into an uneasy stillness and waited. In the distance an owl softened the silence with a gentle *hooooooo*.

Finally she turned back to her task, pushing into the

bottom of the pot with a thick wooden spoon and scraping out the remaining bit of hardening paste. The cauldron clean, she began working it back toward its spot next to the fireplace.

At that moment a loud floorboard creak near the door caused her to spin.

"WHAT BE THIS?"

The bellow startled the cauldron right out of the old woman's hands. She looked up in shock to see a looming shadow peering through the doorway.

"Have mercy!" she cried as the towering intruder stepped into the suddenly much smaller cabin and took stock of the surroundings. Barnes Fullman — mayor of St. Edmund Island — was in full dress, his black wool coat and knee-length breeches barely containing the bulk of him. His prominent white wig brushed the low ceiling as he leaned into the small room, and his ever-present cane dug hard into the old, wooden floor.

"Pray, what is my daughter doing here, and in your bed?"

"Peace, good sir. I pray thee..." Goody Wallace started as she moved between him and the girl.

"Move aside, crone, or I shall surely show you the meaning of a father's wrath!"

"Please, father," the girl mouthed, barely audible through parched lips. "My child desired to come this very eve, but 'twas too early. Goody Wallace has used her physics to great effect."

Her father braced himself against the wall. Only now did the full truth of his daughter's condition begin to sink in.

"Merciful Jesus," he whispered. "My darling Maggy, what's this you say? Be you with child?"

"My lord. If you have mercy in your heart you'd do well to let her rest for the night," the old woman

3

stammered.

The man turned slowly to face her. As their eyes locked she felt her whole body tremble with the same alarming premonitions as before.

"You will all burn," he glowered.

"But thy daughter..."

"No longer!" The hanging pots began to sway. "You are known in this town, Goody Wallace – you who never heeds the church bell or sermon's call. We know full well what you are. You have befouled and cursed my daughter through your dark magicks. Were we in the Old Country I would see thee torn limb from limb."

Turning once more to his daughter, Barnes Fullman paused for a long, torturous moment. Goody Wallace was certain he was about to do something horrible, but to her great relief he finally turned toward the door to leave. Pausing there, he gripped the frame so hard it seemed the timber might crack.

"Be ready, old woman," he whispered without looking back at her, then pounded down the stairs and out into the night.

Moving slowly to a chair, Goody Wallace blew out the candle on the nightstand. In the bed, young Margharet Fullman gave one last moan before finally succumbing to a deep and troubled sleep.

Chapter 2

Present Day. St. Edmund, Massachusetts.

A beam of light cut through the autumn darkness, raising a dance of shadows among the rows of granite, slate and marble. At the beam's source, a thin, trenchcoat-clad figure stood, his black Victorian top hat lifting his height well into the six-foot range. Close around, twenty or so nervous tourists huddled together in the damp cemetery darkness.

"As you see on that elegant tombstone over there, Margharet Fullman passed away on April 23, 1724. She was only nineteen when she left this world."

The tall figure paused, letting the drama of it take root. "Now you'll remember," he pointed his flashlight back down the path "one Hadley Williamson, twenty-three years young, who passed away on the very same day as Margharet. There is no documentation as to the circumstances of either's demise."

Satisfied murmurs among his tour group let Edgar Wilde know he had them in the palm of his hand. He loved a captive audience.

"Given the date, it could possibly be nothing more than simple, tragic coincidence – yellow fever, perhaps. However, some have claimed that they were actually found by Margharet's father — a certain Barnes Fullman — the night before their deaths, caught in a very passionate embrace. Mr. Fullman was clearly a very important man in this town, yet to this day his existence is denied. In fact, the name *Barnes Fullman* isn't found in any of the official historical accounts of this town. Not even a tombstone to remember him by. However –"

At this point in his well-rehearsed and mostly fictional script, Edgar lifted the beam of light to the bottom of his chin, illuminating his face like a ghost.

"– Edgar Wilde Tours isn't afraid to show you the hidden history of the mysterious town of St. Edmund Island. The name *Barnes Fullman* does actually appear in a few scattered public documents of the time period. I am not at liberty to reveal my sources, but I can tell you that I've seen these documents with my own eyes. A few are even in my possession. And finally, of course, there is the unmistakable fact that Margharet and Hadley did somehow end up deceased on the very same day those many years ago. Was there a murder that night? Some sort of cover-up? And if so, why? I'll leave it to you to draw your own conclusions. Let's continue over here."

As the group made their way from the cemetery back to their starting point, their trenchcoat-clad guide spun dramatically to face them once more.

"We are almost at the end of our tour. However, before we disperse I'd like to point out one more curious bit of St. Edmund lore. Cast your eyes toward the bench over there. Yes, that's the one. It may intrigue you to know that the most distinguished horror author, *Edgar Allan Poe*, is said to have sat on that very same bench in September of 1849, penning some lines of verse of which we shall unfortunately never know." Edgar was pleased to see his group draw close in fascination. "Poe fans among you may recall the date of his untimely death as well, and I would like to propose his unsubstantiated visit to St. Edmund as a new and exciting 'missing link' in the mysterious chain of events leading to his unfortunate demise. I will, by the way, have a new Poe-themed tour ready in just a few months' time, in which we will explore this topic in-depth. For any of you planning to visit our lovely, haunted town of St. Edmund again, I hope you will solicit my services further. Again, my name is Edgar Wilde, and no one knows this mysterious New England town as well as..."

"I told you to leave the ghost tours to the professionals!"

A hand swung Edgar around by the elbow, bringing him face-to-face with the plump, elderly figure of Cora Stelton. She wore her period-perfect, black-frilled Victorian mourning attire, decked out to lead her own ghost tour later that evening. She held a lantern high in her other hand; Edgar thought for a moment she was about to beat him with it.

"Do these people know they're being taken by a charlatan?" Her double-chin shook furiously as she looked around at his bemused group. "Do you even know how old this kid is?"

As if shaken suddenly from a trance, the group began to mumble and stir. Quickly noting the unexpected turn of events, Edgar brusquely shook everyone's hands and pushed them off into the night.

"That's the end of the tour, then. I hope you enjoyed your trip back in time tonight. There you go, quickly now. Go find a toasty fire somewhere, and please tell your friends!"

"Yeah, tell them that a 15-year-old kid has been feeding you a bunch of bull!" cried Cora from behind him, causing more rustlings of disapproval from the group. "Edgar, I told you a hundred times. Get off my side of the street and get your butt home where it belongs!" Her thick New England accent sounded like she was spitting gravel.

Side-stepping any further embarrassment, Edgar dashed by Cora's squat form, deftly sliding into one of the small alleyways narrowly dividing the surrounding Colonial structures. His trenchcoat curled behind him as he sidestepped muddy puddles and trash cans, and took off toward home.

A few minutes later, in the privacy of his grand-mother's own light-blue Colonial three-story on Tulane Avenue, Edgar counted the night's take with satisfaction. It had been a good evening overall. There were some genuinely enthused cemetery lovers in the group, which made it delightfully easy to play up to their expectations.

Damn that Stelton woman, though. She had completely soured the mood. There'd be scant return customers from tonight's group. But it was like that sometimes, Edgar conceded as he stashed away his loot.

Tourism was a cut-throat business.

Chapter 3

"The book arrived this morning. Thanks."

Lit by the computer-screen glow, Edgar's face looked especially gaunt and pale. In his hand was his new prize: A rare 1881 first edition of *Beyer's Northeastern Cemetery Symbols and Their Meanings.* It was one of the earliest and least known published works concerning the topic of cemetery iconography. Edgar had been eagerly awaiting its arrival for the past two days.

On the computer screen a weathered, white-goateed face nodded with a condescending satisfaction. Davis "Dade" Alexander was the owner of Dade's Books in Saint Augustine, Florida. He was one of Edgar's favorite sources of rare historical books. He was in his sixties, and he knew his stuff.

"No problem," Dade said. "Keep a lookout for that other book I mentioned, alright? *Quid pro quo.* There's gotta be a copy in your area somewhere. My client has assured me he'll gladly reimburse us both for our troubles. And The Owl won't even talk to me anymore, for some reason."

"I'll discreetly inquire next time I stop in," Edgar said. He wasn't surprised that Dade hadn't made friends with the people at The Owl Bookstore. His gruff manner and slovenly appearance rubbed many in the bookdealing profession the wrong way.

"Thanks for the great find, Dade. You always come

through. You'll have to come to New England sometime and let me give you a tour of the area."

Dade gave him a tired smirk that Edgar translated as a smile, and then the screen went dark.

Edgar let the pages of the book fall gently open. Beautiful. The typestyle was classic: ornate but easily readable. The symbol and design illustrations were all stated on the title page as having been rendered by the author himself, lending an added air of credibility to the work. It was a surprisingly thorough documentation of cemetery marker iconography, from a time when cemeteries were just starting to make the transition from solemn graveyards to the kind of dynamic, rolling cemetery parks where whole families would take picnics and spend happy times with deceased loved ones.

Edgar leaned forward slightly and breathed. *Perfectly musty.*

"Edgar, are you planning to go to school today?" His grandmother's face smiled through the slightly opened door. "Oh my, what have you bought now? That's a lovely book. It looks quite old. Do I want to know how much you paid for it?"

"It's early cemetery iconography stuff. I'll leave it on the bed if you want to look at it later. Be careful with it, though. The spine is a little delicate."

"Since you're so cleverly trying to sidestep my question I suppose you must have paid a pretty penny. You need to haggle, Edgar. I think that Dade fellow takes advantage of your enthusiasm. He'll come down, like any good businessman. It pays to be assertive."

"I do haggle. I got him to come down fifteen bucks on this one."

Aubry chuckled and waved her hand as if to fend away a fly. "Oh, well. I'm sure you do fine. It's none of my business anyway. And at least it's not drugs. Get to school now."

"I'll be down in a second."

Waiting till she was gone, he quickly flipped through the pages. Though Edgar made it a point to regularly add to his cemetery reference library anyway, he had ordered this book for a very specific reason, and he soon found what he'd hoped for.

The star-shaped finial was practically identical to the unusual gravestone icon in a photo on his cellphone.

Illicium verum. Star anise.

Unfortunately, the author had little to say about it, other than its very rare use on cemetery stones. Edgar closed the book, disappointed. He glanced back at the photo of the marker and zoomed out until a name came into view: *Margharet Fullman.* He shook his head and flipped to the other cemetery marker with the same distinct star anise finial: *Hadley Williamson.*

A rare star anise icon, used on two stones very near each other, belonging to two people who died the very same day. It was too weird to be coincidence.

"Grandma, what do you know about star anise?" Edgar said as he hit the bottom step and reached into the foyer for his coat.

His grandmother poked her head through the kitchen door and gave Edgar a funny look.

"Star anise? Dear me and your questions. Edgar, you are going to be so late to school."

"Just quickly, do you know anything about it?"

Aubry toweled her hands dry as she searched for an answer. "Wonderful to cook with. Delightful licorice aroma. Do you remember the chicken I fixed last week? I used a bit in that. Dear me, Edgar, are you preparing a dish?"

"Grandma, when was the last time you saw me cook? Can you think of anything else?"

11

Aubry stared long at Edgar, then sat down. "Let me see. Some say it has medicinal qualities. I've heard it helps digestion, and also acts as a mild sedative. Never experienced that, I must say –"

Edgar's brow furrowed in thought.

"Not what you were hoping for?"

"I'm not sure. Any reason someone would use it as art on a cemetery marker?"

"Oh, dear," she laughed, standing quickly and heading back into the kitchen. "I'm certain I don't have anything useful to say concerning that. Get on to school now."

She watched through the window until Edgar was out of sight, then glanced to the jar on the top shelf. It was full of hard, brown, star-shaped flowers with little shiny seeds embedded in the petals.

A step-stool brought her within reach, and she carefully lowered the jar to the table. It was heavier than she remembered.

Unscrewing the dusty lid, she turned the jar on its side and let the hard, dry star anise flowers roll and tumble out. The pungent aroma embraced her as they scattered across the table, bringing back a swirl of fond memories.

Finally, when enough of the little brown stars had poured out, she reached into the jar and took hold of a small, wooden box that had been concealed within.

"Edgar, Edgar," she shook her head as she blew the light dusting of anise powder off the intricately-carved lid. "You and your cemeteries. What have you stumbled on now?"

Chapter 4

"Class, may I remind you to show a little respect?" Mrs. Dickerson warbled her octaves like a farm hen. "I don't want to have to start handing out detentions, and I'm sure you don't want me to either. Please be polite and let Mr. Wilde continue."

Mrs. Dickerson's dreaded over-the-glasses glare was now aimed at her entire fifth-period history class. Edgar waited patiently as the snickering subsided, hands resting flat on the report he was only three paragraphs into presenting. His eyes accidentally caught sight of resident bully Jacob Mason five rows back — reclined straight as a board, arms crossed tight, giving Edgar an unblinking eyeful of *kick-your-ass*. He was the only student apparently not amused.

"Thank you, Mrs. Dickerson," Edgar turned back to his audience. "The fact that people used to have picnics in cemeteries — that they actually sat in the grass next to their dead parents or grandparents, eating together and even playing games — is hard to imagine. But only a hundred years ago it was quite acceptable, even encouraged. By the beginning of the 20th century a new style of cemetery had emerged. Instead of morbid church grounds with cemetery stones designed to remind passers-by of their fleeting mortality, we now see the arrival of quite stylish and popular park-like cemeteries, designed specifically for the living to enjoy. This is also when you see some truly remarkable, museum-quality statuary…"

"That's for sure! There's a wicked-hot angel statue over at Greenwood that's got 'em hanging right out there in the open –" Jacob accentuated his point by cupping both hands to his chest.

"Jacob Mason!" Mrs. Dickerson's voice shook as the room exploded into a riot of guffaws. "I will not have it! You will find your way to the principal's office now, and I will see you there shortly."

"I'm just saying!" Jacob protested as he made his way toward the door. "*Ed-Gore* here may not appreciate it, of course, but Greenwood's got some sweet marble ass behind its gate. Wish he'd give a report on those for a fucking change – ."

"Language!" Mrs. Dickerson squawked as he snaked out the door and the room collapsed into renewed laughter. In the meantime, Edgar rolled up his mostly-unread script and found his chair. There was a moment in almost every one of Mrs. Dickerson's classes when a chaotic crescendo would be reached, and instead of confronting it she would retreat to her desk in quiet defeat. She'd wait for the bell to chime, pretend to grade papers and tests while the class tailspun into a cacophony of gossip and laughter.

This was certainly that moment. Edgar slid into the chair and pulled out pen and paper to doodle the final minutes of class away.

He was already into the hall by the time the bell finished ringing, reaching his locker just as the mob of students poured out *en-masse* from their classes.

"Nice presentation, *Ed-Gore*. What a surprise, more cemetery shit." Edgar didn't even need to look behind him to know it was Amanda Barnes. Edgar still remembered Amanda from fifth grade, spitting gum in his hair from the window of a school bus. Nothing had changed since. "Have you considered giving – oh, I don't know – a report on something normal for a change?"

He closed his locker and turned. No surprise. Accompanying Amanda were her very own posse, Becky Carr and Shelby Emerson. The three owned a whole back corner of Mrs. Dickerson's history class; Amanda had actually been the one who'd originally interrupted his presentation and triggered the downward spiral of the class.

Edgar stole a glance at Shelby Emerson. He'd recently found himself glancing at her at odd moments, noticing her curly, strawberry-blonde hair and the way she laughed, and the curve of her legs. The fact that she talked way too much about nothing and had distressingly bad taste in friends quickly shot down any possibility of something ever happening between them. Not that he ever thought about that. Still, she continued to ping on the edge of his radar like a torpedo-loaded sub.

"I thought your report was sort of interesting, what there was of it," Shelby laughed. He glanced away, avoiding her apologetic smile. "Maybe Mrs. Dickerson will let you finish it on Monday."

"Umm, thanks."

"God, I hope not," Becky said. "My favorite part was when you stopped talking!" This caused all three to snort and giggle as they departed.

"And thank you, ladies, for your support," Edgar said quietly as he turned to gather his things. What a relief the weekend had finally arrived.

Chapter 5

"That smells incredible. Dark roast today?"

"Sumatra!" Sarah the Barista sang out as she handed him his order.

"*Gesundheit,*" Edgar replied, scooping his change off the counter.

"Sumatra's my absolute favorite," she continued, entirely missing his joke. "The fresh-ground beans are roasted over in Fall River. I shave the cinnamon straight from the stick, too! I know you like cinnamon."

Her last comment was accompanied by a suggestive wink that brought Edgar's cup of cinnamon coffee to a screeching halt in front of his lips. Noticing his hesitation, Sarah the Barista's dimply, eager smile melted into a horrified frown.

"Is it too hot? Oh, no! I'm sorry, Edgar. I try to make sure it's not scalding, but sometimes it's hard to tell. You want some ice? Here, we have ice. Just give me a moment –" She was already moving toward the back room before Edgar could raise a hand to protest.

"No, thank you, Sarah. I'm good. Really!" To prove it he took a large sip, and regretted it immediately as his mouth ignited in flames. He hoped she hadn't seen the sudden anguish on his face as her head poked around the corner. As much as her moments of rainbow bliss were a joy to behold, Sarah the Barista's sudden descents into self-flagellation could be horrible to witness.

"Are you sure?"

"Mmm-hmmm!" he shook his head vigorously, causing strands of black hair to fall out from under his top hat. "So, umm, cold walk to work this morning, Sarah?"

"I had to wear my thermal underwear," she gushed as if she'd been waiting for Edgar to ask. "Still got it on under all of this!" Before Edgar could look away, Sarah the Barista was striking a number of odd, provocative poses as she modeled her burgundy-and-green uniform for him. This unexpected, mortifying display of polyester-wrapped chub and dimples caused him to begin to back slowly away from the counter.

"That's great, Sarah," he blurted, fumbling desperately for the doorknob. "I mean, I'm glad you're keeping warm. Okay, then. Don't take any wooden nickels. I'm sorry, gotta run! See you next Saturday!"

A few blocks away Edgar finally slowed, coming to a stop outside of Jenkins Bistro. Was it just him or was Sarah the Barista getting weirder? He wasn't sure if what he'd just witnessed was simply a case of over-caffeination, or maybe the beginnings of a mental breakdown. Worse case scenario: She was actually flirting with him. Edgar closed his eyes tight, trying to squeeze the image out of his mind. He'd need to reevaluate his Saturday morning ritual if this kept up.

Holding the hot cup between his hands, he watched as the first brave tourists tentatively worked their way along the cobblestones of Pine Street. Hundreds of years of feet, hooves, wooden carriage wheels, and automobile tread had created deep, permanent ruts and frozen crests in the road; it was a delight to watch people trying to navigate it during the winter months.

Taking another sip of the scalding, rich brew (which his numb tongue could no longer feel), Edgar finally set out towards his next destination. He wasn't looking forward to the visit; doing field work for Dade when The Owl Bookstore had already cut off contact with him made Edgar feel like some sort of spy. He wasn't doing anything wrong, really. But it didn't feel right, either. Felicia wouldn't be happy to know Edgar was book-scouting for Dade.

Chapter 6

"Edgar! Staying warm?"

Felicia Thompson, owner of The Owl Bookstore, looked up and smiled as Edgar entered. She was African-American, wheelchair-bound, and one of the most exuberantly pleasant people in all of St. Edmund. Edgar found her perpetual warmth uncomfortably disarming.

Distracted by the new book arrivals on the front shelf, Edgar gave her a quick smile as he started to peruse the selections.

"Oh, I've found something you might be interested in." Felicia pulled out a tome that Edgar recognized instantly.

"Mrs. Thompson! That's an early *Psalm* book."

"From 1744," she smiled. "Can you believe that someone was using this as a decoration on a piano?" Her fingers danced lightly along the ornate leather cover. "Yours if you want it. We can negotiate later."

Edgar's first-glance appraisal of the rare book left him mentally salivating. It was museum-quality. He considered his bank account, emptied by his recent purchase from Dade. He knew Felicia would give him a tremendous deal, but it would take quite a few cemetery tours to rebuild his funds to a place where he could afford it.

"Mrs. Thompson, I don't know –"

"Just think about it a bit," she said. "I know you were on the lookout for one. I'll keep it in the safe for you."

"Thanks, Mrs. Thompson. While we're on the subject, any new leads concerning that other book I asked you about, the one with the recipes and herbal stuff?" It was the closest thing to a smooth segue that he could have hoped for.

"No, this is all that's come in recently, I'm afraid. I'll certainly be sure to let you know if I hear of anything." Her smile made Edgar feel she knew exactly on whose behalf he was inquiring. He nodded sheepishly.

"How is your calligraphy coming?" she asked. "I loved the sample you showed me. It's a lost art form, you know. Not many people doing it these days, now that computers have made everything so easy. Nice to see you taking such an interest."

Edgar was grateful for the change of subject. "I think I'm finally getting some of the subtleties down. By the way, the parchment you gave me is perfect; it really holds the ink."

"I was thinking we might frame some of your finished pages and hang them around the store. That is, if you're interested in some artistic exposure? And that way your grandmother might come pay me a visit as well. Tell her it's been awhile."

Chapter 7

Edgar was still riding high on the thought of his calligraphy being displayed as he approached Christmas Jingle. A sparkly, yuletide-filled store, it was dedicated year-round to Christmas decorations. He couldn't for his life figure out how the place stayed in business.

The owner, Gertrude Hedgewick, glanced up from her morning sweeping of the tiny section of sidewalk as he walked by.

"Morning, Mrs. Hedgewick," Edgar said politely. He never expected a reply, and she never gave one.

Except for today.

"Heard you were out bothering everyone again last night."

The shock of her gravelly voice brought Edgar to a standstill. Had she ever spoken to him before?

"Excuse me?" He turned slowly.

"Cemetery tour," her voice rasped. "Telling lies to all those tourists. You should mind your business."

Edgar felt a chill in his bones, a cold beyond anything the weather could throw at him. He drew himself tall.

"My tours are entertaining and well-researched, I assure you."

"Research!" she scoffed. "St. Edmund Island doesn't benefit by you stirring up ashes, Mister Wilde. We don't appreciate you poking around."

"This is my town too, Mrs. Hedgewick."

"Your family has been trouble for as far back as I can recall. Heed my warning and keep your nose out of things you don't understand."

Before Edgar could respond, the gnarled Hedgewick woman threw down her broom and slammed the door hard behind her as she went back inside.

Edgar took a moment to recover from the unexpected verbal assault, then finally picked up the forlorn broom from the sidewalk and leaned it gently against the door.

Two old women in as many days giving me an earful, he thought as he continued to the library. *What are the odds?*

Chapter 8

"I don't understand what's with you."

Edgar was deep in concentration, converting microfilm archives into digital images at the town library. He often dug up bits of forgotten town history from the archives that he could use in his tours, and he'd just struck paydirt.

On his screen, a copy of a splotchy, faded leaflet announced a town meeting dated April 23, 1724, at the Primitive Baptist Church. Edgar knew of the existence of the church; it had once stood just outside of town, but weather and arson had taken care of it more than a century ago. The property was now home to an auto body shop.

"You are always wearing that freaky hat. You're, like, so Victorian. Is that the right word? And *Wilde*. What kind of name is *Wilde*? That can't be your real name. Did you make that up just to be weird?"

The details were maddeningly vague. At the bottom of the flyer was a reference to the organizer of the meeting — a certain *Mayor B.F.* That was interesting. And was it simply a coincidence that the date of the town meeting over 250 years ago happened to be the very same day his cemetery-tour mainstays — Margharet Fullman and Hadley Williamson — had mysteriously died?

"Can you do an English accent? Are you trying to be English?"

Edgar finally raised his head from the microfilm viewer, giving the girl across from him a dark glance.

"A little quiet, please?"

"Yes! The ghost finally speaks!" Shelby Emerson spun her chair around three times in victory, flipping her thick, curly mop of strawberry-blonde hair. Rolling her chair over to Edgar's table, she propped her elbows on its surface, chin resting on hands. She ignored the intentionally loud sigh Edgar gave in response. "So what are you working on? You're here every weekend. Are you actually working, or just reading stuff? It looks easy enough."

"I'm archiving old microfilm," Edgar replied. "It's nothing special. Really."

"I'm bored. Tell me about your ghost tours. Have you really seen ghosts in the cemetery? Or is it all made up?"

"They're cemetery tours, not ghost tours," Edgar already regretted having opened his mouth at all. He printed out a copy of his newfound discovery and began packing his bag.

"I don't believe in ghosts."

"Awesome," he zipped his satchel. "Stick with that."

"But have you actually seen any? I saw an orb once, but it turned out to be a streetlight."

"People see what they want," he said neutrally as he donned his long, black overcoat.

"Are you leaving?" Shelby quickly slid into her shiny black leather coat. "I'm actually done, too."

Edgar paused. "Shelby, what are you doing?"

"It's time to go, isn't it? So I'm leaving then. That's what people do when it's time to go."

"Are you sure you want to be seen leaving with *me?*"

"I don't care. But stay here if it bothers you so much."

Edgar rolled his eyes as he grabbed his bag and they both headed for the door.

Chapter 9

The delicate, white cotton curtains billowed in the icy breeze of the open kitchen window, like ghosts dancing on the air.

Aubry Wilde's small, elegant hands rested atop the wooden box's locked lid. The ornately-engraved dark wood made her fingers look like fragile glass. The old box hadn't been opened for many years now, but she could still recall the aroma — undercurrents of cedar and pine, along with the intense, ever-present note of licorice.

Funny, the things we carry with us in this world — the many things that never let go.

Cora Stelton had stopped by unannounced earlier that morning. She'd arrived bearing a delicious-looking sweet potato casserole, still hot from the oven. She also gave her a message concerning Edgar.

Her friend's alarm over Edgar's curiosity brought a mischievous smile to Aubry's thin lips as she traced the edge of the box with a finger. She had known Cora for many years, even serving with her on the St. Edmund Historical Society committee. Her stout friend had always been easily given to panic, but Aubry had never seen her like this.

Aubry gazed out the open window, the winter air sending tingles through her whole body as it swept past. Soon there would be snow.

Chapter 10

The chilly bay winds whipped Edgar's thick overcoat all about. When he'd left the library, he certainly hadn't expected Shelby to follow. But there she was, tagging close behind. How she'd gotten him to start ranting about Barnes Fullman was beyond him. He held his top hat to his head and squinted as strands of black hair bit at his face.

Shelby matched his quick pace. "So Fullman doesn't even have a tombstone in the cemetery? But maybe he moved away or something. Anyway, why does it matter? So no one remembers him — maybe he was a mediocre mayor. Do people really pay you to talk about this stuff? You know, my mom's all upset about you. She was going on about something Mrs. Stelton said to her last night — something about that Fullman guy and how you should be minding your own business."

Edgar came to a stop. "Really? *Barnes Fullman* is what Mrs. Stelton's upset about?"

"I was upstairs listening."

"I don't get it – why would that make her upset? The Historical Society has no trace of him. *Nobody* knows about him. Why should Mrs. Stelton even care that I mention him on my tours?"

"I heard her say she's afraid you're going to open some sort of *Pandora's Box.*"

"She really said that?"

"Can we keep walking? I am freezing my ass off."

"Oh, sorry. But I found evidence that places Mayor Barnes Fullman at a town meeting on April 23, 1724," Edgar said as they picked up their pace. "Now two people died that very same day, which isn't so strange given the time period and the waves of yellow fever rolling through. However, what is strange is that one of them was most likely his very own daughter. There's some kind of secret or lost bit of St. Edmund history just waiting to be discovered. And while the town may have forgotten whatever it was that happened, it seems Mrs. Stelton has not. She obviously thinks I'm about to uncover something very important."

He glanced over to her, expecting her to be checking out her nails or something. To his surprise her blue eyes were still focused on him.

"That is so cool! You should let me help you."

"Help me? Shelby, I..." Edgar broke off as he noticed the lanky cemetery caretaker, Corinthian Harknell, waving at them from McKreary's Tavern.

"Who's that?" Shelby asked.

"Come on," Edgar took Shelby by the arm as they crossed the cobblestones to say hello.

Chapter 11

If it was possible, Corinthian looked even more English than usual in his tweed jacket and yellow and green-striped scarf. His handshake with Edgar was muffled by fingerless, woolen gloves that matched his colorful scarf.

"Edgar! I see you've got a friend with you this lovely Saturday!"

"Corinthian, this is Shelby. She's an acquaintance from school."

"Delighted to meet you, dear girl," He bowed dramatically over Shelby's hand. "And what a rose you are. Is this not the face that launched a thousand ships?"

Edgar rolled his eyes.

Corinthian continued, giving Edgar a toothy grin. "And lucky you to be on her arm on this beautiful day!"

"I'm not –!" Edgar began to protest as Corinthian held up his hand and continued.

"Sometimes you must step away from the garden to properly see the rose in your midst, wouldn't you agree?"

"What rose?" Edgar said. Meanwhile, Shelby was quickly becoming a melty pool of wax.

"*How does it happen that birds sing, that snow melts, that the rose unfolds?*" Corinthian waxed. "*A kiss, and all was said.*"

"Victor Hugo, Corinthian? You're actually quoting a Frenchman? I can't believe I've lived to hear it."

"Hugo may have suffered being born French, but he

had the heart of a Brit!" Corinthian's wiry, white eyebrows bristled in a fervent scowl. "You cannot help where you are born, by God, but you must certainly rise above it! Now then," he smiled warmly, "join me for a drink?"

"This is like a scene from *Lord of the Rings*," Shelby said as they entered McKreary's and slid into a roomy and well-worn booth that smelled of cigars. "How do you even see your glass?"

Corinthian gestured to the barkeep, giving him the tip of an imaginary cap.

"Shelby, what are you doing watching *Lord of the Rings?*" Edgar gaped. "Isn't that against your cheerleading code or something?"

"I'm not a cheerleader, doofus. Anyway, what makes you think I don't like fantasy? I read Tolkien years before the movies came out."

"So, Shelby, tell us more about you, then," Corinthian leaned in with an amorous gaze. "I remember your mom from church choir many years back. Sorry to hear about your father, by the way. He was a wonderful fellow. Knew a thing or two about science, as I recall."

"Thanks," she mumbled, looking down at a knot in the thick oak table.

"And now you're one of us, what do you think of our little mystery, eh? Surely Edgar has enlightened you. He thinks of little else these days."

"Well, I . . ." she started.

"Corinthian, she's not 'one of us.' She's just hanging out," Edgar interrupted.

"Oh I see," Corinthian said nonchalantly as a pint of very dark beer arrived in front of him. "*Ahhh,* there we are. Now we can properly begin. Hold on to your seats, my dears –" He took a deep swig from his pint, then reached into the tattered leather bag beside him and dramatically pulled out an old book, letting it fall on the table. "As I have access to all the town mortuary records, I thought you might want to peruse this little date-of-death ledger I happened upon. It's a record of all the St. Edmund deceased from 1703 to 1872."

Edgar's eyes grew wide. "That would include almost everyone in the old cemetery, including –" He felt his pulse jump.

Corinthian opened the ledger to the page marked *April 23, 1724.*

"Look at that," Edgar whispered. "There they are, right next to each other." On two lines, one below the next, were the names *Margharet Fullman* and *Hadley Williamson.*

"Indeed. And I found something in this little ledger that may intrigue you even further."

"You found Fullman!" Shelby cried out. Edgar gave Corinthian an apologetic, bemused shake of the head.

"You'd think Barnes Fullman would be in here some-where, wouldn't you?" Corinthian squinted his eyes at her mischievously. "And I'd be inclined to agree. So I'll be curious as to what you make of this, then."

He flipped forward a few years to 1732. His finger dragged down the page, stopping near the bottom.

Ophelia Goodwicke.

"You know it, of course," Corinthian nudged Edgar.

"Of course. The Zinc Oxide Lady."

"Ophelia Goodwicke? That's a weird name," Shelby said. "So what's a *Zinc Oxide Lady?* Sounds like some sort of superhero."

Edgar scrolled through his cellphone photos of all the monuments in St. Edmund Cemetery, whirling through the parade of weathered granite and marble until he finally found the one he was looking for. Then he slid the phone over to her. The glowing image revealed an ornate, weathered, bluish-gray tombstone.

"Has it been painted or something? It doesn't look normal."

Edgar leaned in, enlarging the photo for her. "It's made of a metal called zinc oxide. It was very popular back in the late 1800s. Mass-produced. Ophelia's is the only stone in the entire cemetery made out of the stuff. That's how she earned her title."

"Is there anything more distasteful than assembly-line grave markers?" Corinthian spat. "They're actually hollow on the inside, you know. You can hear the echo when you tap it. And they're notoriously brittle with age. Absolutely disgraceful."

"You guys know way too much about this stuff," Shelby laughed.

"My dear, life doesn't even begin until you start exploring the world of cemeteries," Corinthian swigged a deep gulp of beer. "All of human experience and wisdom can be found in any one of your quaint countryside grave-yards. Personally, I can think of nowhere more tranquil or enlightening."

Shelby rolled her eyes. "I'll wait my turn, thanks."

"Ah, well," Corinthian smiled. "There's plenty of time to convince you otherwise."

"Good luck with that one! So, I'm just going to ask a stupid question: how did you resolve the problem with the dates?"

"Problem?"

"Didn't you say the zinc oxide thing was popular in the 1800s?"

"Indeed," Corinthian said.

"But not the 1700s?"

"Certainly not. Zinc oxide wasn't used at all for the manufacture of cemetery markers until –" Corinthian stopped mid-exposition as the truth hit him.

"Until much later," Shelby finished his sentence. "That's what I'm saying! So how did you resolve that inconsistency?"

Corinthian caught Edgar's dumbstruck gaze and began to chuckle. They'd both missed it. The Ophelia marker was a hundred years too early for it to be made out of zinc oxide.

"It appears we're still working on that one, my dear," Corinthian bluffed. Edgar shook his head, mortified that Shelby had been the one to catch such an obvious clue.

"Well you guys are suddenly quiet," Shelby said. "Anyway, her name is right here in the ledger — *Date of death: 1732* — so there must be some explanation."

"Agreed," Corinthian slowly ran a finger around the top of his pint glass. "In the meantime, I think I've found something else to occupy your acute powers of observation. Take a moment to examine her name closely. Notice anything unusual?"

Edgar leaned in. This one was a no-brainer. "The writing's different. Though similar in handwriting to the other entries, there are obviously telltale differences. It's almost like –" He looked up at Corinthian, who was watching him intently. "This is not the original name. *Ophelia Goodwicke* was written at a later date."

"Like the marker, which was made with a material not yet used on the inscribed date," Corinthian said, giving a nod to Shelby. "Our lady Ophelia has apparently traveled back in time, intentionally inserting herself into the year 1732."

"And erased whoever was originally on the line," Edgar said as he examined the page closely. "Look here — someone has scraped away the original writing with a knife. There was another name here."

"This is crazy," Shelby crossed her arms. "I mean, whoever's name was there first didn't *un*-die, right?"

37

Edgar rested the light flat on the page to better see any subtle details. As he slowly moved his eyes along the paper, he gasped as a familiar name suddenly lifted from the milky shadows of the parchment, reclaiming its long-forgotten place in history.

"It's Fullman," he said in astonishment. "This is the lost record of Barnes Fullman's death."

Chapter 12

April 23, 1724. St. Edmund Island, Massachusetts.

"God be with you," Reverend Allen nodded warmly at the families entering the packed, little church, and then poked his head in the door. He'd never seen such a crowd.

God grant these decent townsfolk divine guidance today!

A booming voice drew his attention as he stepped into the main vestibule. Mayor Barnes Fullman, white-wigged and generous of girth, had been using his pulpit for the past two hours to deliver his message to the assembled throng.

"Righteous ones, take note of your missing kinfolk today," Fullman continued. "Even now, up on the hill overlooking the bay, they are gathered unto Satan's spell. How in God's name do you sit idly by, allowing all to be swept up into the Devil's foul purpose?" He pounded his walking stick hard on the reverberant wooden floors, emphasizing each point. "There are seven heads of the snake — seven souls already taken — right up there on that cursed hill. Who knows what horror they cast over this town? Are we to be damned for their salacious deviance?"

Reverend Allen could feel the sweat gathering on his upper lip. Despite the open doors and windows, the room was slowly turning into an oven of hot, stagnant air. Fullman's oratory was passionate and puritanical beyond anything the reverend had ever preached, as hot as the room itself.

And it was gathering momentum.

Beads of sweat found their way down the reverend's neck as he worked to maintain his stone demeanor. He swayed slightly in the pungent air as Fullman continued his vitriolic diatribe.

"My friends, God has revealed the venom poisoning our township. With one decisive action we may cast a blow to the Devil himself!"

The murmurs increased, rolling from one side of the church to the other.

In his hand, Mayor Fullman held high the book he'd been quoting from throughout the day: John Hale's popular *A Modest Enquiry Into the Nature of Witchcraft*. The book — written by a chief participant of the recent Salem trials to the north — presented itself as an objective, fair account of the methods used to rid the town of the Devil, and as a guide for others who might need the same kind of insight.

The helpless reverend looked toward the rafters, silently imploring God for guidance.

"Strike now!" Mayor Fullman cried, bringing the crowd to its feet. "The Devil waits there on the hill. May this gathering of souls be cursed if we do not face him this very night!"

Reverend Allen pressed into the wall as the gathering-turned-mob pushed past him, out into the dark. From his vantage point he could easily see out the door, straight up the hill less than a mile's distance away. Up there, he knew, a number of unsuspecting souls were about to meet a most horrific end.

Chapter 13

Present Day. St. Edmund, Massachusetts.

"Left your broom leaning outside the door, old woman."

Gertrude lay down the balsam garland. She hadn't heard Cora enter the store. Her friend was all jet-black beading and ruffles, ready for the night's cemetery tours. Pure Victorian melodrama, Gertrude thought in disdain.

"I've got other things on my mind than a stupid broom."

"It's wicked bad to misplace your broom!" Cora said, deadly serious.

"Oh, for Heaven's sake!" Gertrude tossed her hazy bifocals to the table.

Cora sat down, resting the broom across her lap. "So, what about the boy?" She enunciated each word for emphasis.

"Talked to him earlier today, actually. He's nothing but an arrogant brat. You can thank Aubry for that."

"I'm tired of being skunked by a kid! He's stealing clients, doing tours in the cemetery, acting like he's the expert!" Cora stood in frustration.

"*That's* what you're worried about?"

Cora waved off Gertrude's attitude, remaining silent as she walked back and forth along a seam in the red wall to wall.

"Anyway, if you're going to pace like that you might

as well get me a mocha latte from next door," Gertrude slid a small pile of coins in Cora's direction.

As Cora took the change, Gertrude added, "Watch them — sometimes they skimp on the cinnamon. They're cheap over there."

"I'll make sure," Cora said sharply. "I won't tell them it's for you."

"Be sure to bring me my change, dear!"

It was so like Gertrude to assign ridiculous tasks to her, Cora steamed as she worked the loose change angrily in her hand. She had more important things to do than to run errands for that prude!

"Mocha latte be damned!" she spat on the sidewalk as she abandoned her assignment and pursued an altogether different task.

Chapter 14

Corinthian took a satisfied swig of beer.

"I still don't see it," Shelby lowered her head closer to the page.

"Here," Edgar gently guided her hand across the name. "Look closely where you feel the ridges."

"I just see scratches."

"Do you seriously not see that 'B' right there?" Edgar replied in exasperation.

"Maybe if you would get out of my light!"

"Children, children," Corinthian soothed. "Suffice it to say, someone clearly went to great efforts to remove the late, great Barnes Fullman from this ledger. But why?"

Edgar gazed into his phone screen at the picture of the Ophelia Goodwicke marker. He still couldn't believe he'd never picked up on the discrepancy with the dates and the material used to make the marker. He glanced at Shelby in begrudging admiration. She had seen it straight away.

"Oh, there it is! I see it now!" Shelby looked up from the page, victorious. "So, Ophelia Goodwicke can't be a real person then, can she?"

"I don't think so, love," Corinthian said. "Nothing more than a very clever conceit."

"*Underneath*," Edgar repeated, still looking at the image of the marker on his phone. Could it really be? "Come on!" he yelled as he bolted for the door.

"Wait, lad!" Corinthian shuffled for his wallet. "I haven't even paid the tab yet!"

Chapter 15

"Dude, the cemetery's not going anywhere!" Shelby yelled. She couldn't tell if Edgar was actually out of earshot or if he was just ignoring her. He was two blocks ahead and had just turned onto Mission Street.

Toward the cemetery.

"Damn it. The lad's hot on the trail!" Corinthian wheezed.

"Is this something you two do regularly?" Shelby said as she ran up to keep pace with him. "How did you two meet, anyway?"

"I first met Edgar when he was eight," Corinthian said as he slowed down to catch his breath. "His grandmother, Aubry, was walking him around town, introducing him to everyone. He'd just moved up from Florida, you see. The first thing the boy asked me was if I could show him a dead body. Can you imagine that? A dead body! Aubry apologized, and then Edgar walked right up and said, 'I hope I have not harmed our future friendship with my inadvertent rudeness.'

"Such manners! That was my first encounter with Edgar. I must admit I have grown such a fondness for the boy in the years since, he has become almost like a son to me. Oh dear, I've lost sight of him now."

"So this cemetery thing is your fault then!" Shelby laughed as they turned the corner and entered the arching gate of St. Edmund Cemetery. Even from the entrance they could see Edgar's black line of a silhouette, standing near the very back, right in front of the Ophelia Goodwicke grave marker.

Edgar stood quietly, mentally mapping every detail. Bold, sharp-edged Victorian-age letters arched over the top of the flat, blue-gray metal face, spelling out the name *Ophelia Goodwicke*. Underneath, the date of death: *1732*.

Below that, an epitaph was etched:

*Pointing Toward the Heavens, Touching to Avail,

Penetrate Thy Curtain, and Lift Thy Mortal Veil.*

At either top corner was a classic bit of artwork: A hand rising out of a cloud with index finger pointing upward.

"Thanks for letting us catch up," Shelby said tartly as she walked past Edgar and knelt down by the marker. Rapping it with her knuckles, a deep *toooommm* reverberated within.

"You were certainly right, Corinthian. That's creepy."

"It's just hollow," Edgar said.

"Still creepy. Something could be in there."

"Like?"

"It just sounds very creepy. What if there's something dead in there?"

"Shelby, it's a grave. There *is* something dead in there."

"I mean on the inside of the marker. This thing is the perfect place for something creepy to be hidden. Isn't messing with graves some sort of crime against God or something? I mean, look at the warning: *Pointing Toward the Heavens*. You can't just –" She trailed off suddenly, gazing at the epitaph.

"Shelby, what?" Edgar said.

"*Touching To Avail*," she whispered. "Do either of you know where these verses come from?"

"No clue, I'm afraid," Corinthian breathed deeply, still shaky from the run. "I don't think it's from the Bible, though it certainly sounds it."

Shelby leaned closer to the marker. "I don't think it's from anything. I think someone made these verses up."

"Shelby, why would you possibly think that?" Edgar asked. "You have nothing to base that deduction on."

"Read it carefully, doofus," she said as she brought her finger up to one of the small pointing hand symbols. "*Pointing toward the heavens*. What else could it be but the hands?"

Looking at Edgar mischievously, she gave the pointing finger symbol a gentle push. Deep inside the marker they could hear the sound of metal rubbing against metal.

"*Touching to avail*," Edgar said, stunned. "The hands are buttons!"

Shelby stood up and danced a victory jig around him. "That's two for me, I believe!"

Corinthian rubbed his gloved hands together as he paced. "A secret button, hidden in plain sight. Brilliant! You've certainly earned your keep, Shelby. Top notch."

"And *Lift Thy Mortal Veil*," Edgar mused. "It's got to be a reference to the zinc oxide shell —"

Edgar was about to say more when something in the distance caught his eye. At the far corner of the cemetery, standing dead still, was a squat, black figure.

Chapter 16

"He asked for it again."

Felicia watched people strolling by her bookshop window as she held the phone close. She'd hesitated to call Aubry, but there was nothing else to do.

"Well, you don't have it, do you?"

"Of course not. But how did he even hear about it? And poor Edgar, you should have seen him doing that man's dirty work when he was in earlier. I have half a mind to call Dade Alexander and give him some choice words."

"Felicia, take a nice, deep breath," Aubry soothed. "The bookdealer is not the most agreeable fellow, but I don't think he means Edgar harm. My guess is a third party commissioned him to find the book and he simply asked Edgar for help in scouting around for it."

"Maybe. But why would someone looking for *that* book pick a bookdealer located all the way down in Florida?"

"Perhaps Mr. Alexander has some special inside edge that makes him an ideal choice."

"Inside edge? Aubry, the man is slovenly, rude, and a second-rate bookseller besides. I have a hard time even imagining how he's able to stay in business with his customer service skills."

"But he does know certain people, doesn't he?"

Felicia felt the hairs on her arms rise.

"Edgar? You think Dade's friendship with Edgar is why Dade was commissioned to find the book? Oh, Aubry, what has that boy gotten himself into? You know there are those who would –"

At that moment the bell above the door announced a customer, causing Felicia to jump. Composing herself, she smiled at the elderly couple and motioned that she'd be off the phone soon.

"I know, dear, I know. And it appears Edgar has stirred up quite a nest of hornets with his little cemetery tour hobby as well. Cora even stopped by for some tea, if you can imagine. Edgar's been talking about *Barnes Fullman* in his tours. That can only mean he's found the name in his research somewhere."

Felicia glanced back at her customers. They were in the cooking section, reading up on Italian cuisine.

"I've got to let you go. Keep me updated, okay?"

"Okay, dear. You had better stock up, by the way. I do believe a snowstorm's headed our way."

Chapter 17

Cora Stelton was veiled and enshrouded in corseted, black Victorian mourning attire, looking every bit the cemetery ghost as she approached the trio.

"Mr. Harknell," she said. "I see you managed to get the boy involved in your foolishness."

He smiled innocently in response. "Mrs. Stelton, a delight. To what do I owe the honor of seeing your lovely countenance?"

"Beware the snake's tongue," Cora spat out. "Who do you think you are, Harknell?" Edgar and Shelby glanced at each other. Corinthian, however, seemed unshaken.

"Mrs. Stelton, this is a public cemetery, and I am merely its appointed custodian. My lot is a humble one. However, please do recall that it is at my discretion that you run your very profitable tours here."

"The nerve!" Mrs. Stelton hissed. "You owe me, Harknell. Don't think I've forgotten what's owed."

"That may be," Corinthian leaned close to her ear. "Either way, dear Cora, today is not your day to collect."

The old woman shrunk back from Corinthian with a contemptuous glare. Then she abruptly redirected her venom at Edgar.

"The Ophelia Goodwicke cemetery marker is an exclusive part of my tour, Mr. Wilde. I've got it in my pamphlet! You'd do well to stay clear!"

Then, giving them all a final, threatening glare, she took hold of her hem and departed.

"Spooky," Shelby whispered once she was out of earshot. "For an old lady caged in crinoline she moves surprisingly fast."

"Bitter old hag," Corinthian said. "Would you believe she was once crowned winner of the St. Edmund Island Beauty Contest?"

"Corinthian, really?" Shelby raised her eyebrows in disbelief.

"No, not really," Corinthian chuckled. "But she could have. Long ago she had a sparkling personality and a contagious sense of humor. You'd be surprised to know there were quite a few of us lads who competed for that girl's attention. Ah, well. Time does reveal all things," Corinthian rapped on the top of the tombstone. "However, the secrets here will have to wait, I'm afraid. No doubt we're being watched."

Edgar had come to the same conclusion as soon as he'd seen Mrs. Stelton, but he couldn't seem to move from the spot.

Corinthian noticed Edgar's pained expression. "Come on, lad. Fortune favors the patient. The curtain shall be lifted soon enough." He winked at Edgar, then bowed to Shelby. "Madam, thank you for your assistance today. I hope you'll grace us with your cleverness again."

"Are you kidding?" Shelby said, grabbing Corinthian's arm. "You better not do anything further without me. Promise!"

"My dear, you're a part of the team now, aren't you? Your mother won't be exactly thrilled by your choice of company, mind you, but I am honored."

As the three made their way back out of the cemetery, Edgar turned and thought for a moment he saw movement in the direction of the Ophelia marker. He stopped, causing his friends to turn as well.

"Don't let that bitter old woman get to you," Corinthian said. "She's probably just retracing her steps, seeing if we left any clues."

"You think she —"

"No! I'm sure she was too far away to detect our unusual discovery."

"But what if she finds out about the buttons on her own?" Shelby said.

"What was she even doing there?" Edgar said, turning to Corinthian. "I get that she's a tour guide and trying to protect her trade. But why was she so worked up about the Ophelia marker? She seemed almost frightened."

"Why indeed?" Corinthian smiled. "She was following us, clearly. I can't say why that marker means so much to her, but we certainly seem to have made it onto someone's radar."

Chapter 18

"Edgar, may I come in?"

"Sure, grandma," Edgar said, resting the quill on the ink bottle. He'd been hunched over his desk, working diligently at his calligraphy in an attempt to keep his mind off the incredible discovery he and his friends had made at the cemetery earlier that day.

It wasn't working. He had half a mind to grab a flashlight and run back out there that instant.

Aubry leaned over his work.

"Oh, that's beautiful," she smiled. "You really have improved."

"Felicia said she might like to frame some of my pages and display them at The Owl."

"My! That would be quite a feather. Felicia is such a dear. So, how is school going?"

"Fine." He gave her a smile meant to reassure.

"Edgar, do you know how old this community is? How long it's been around?" He gave her a confused look in response.

"Yes, of course you do!" Aubry laughed, patting his knee. "You probably know more about St. Edmund than anyone else I know."

"What is it, grandma?"

"Lots of people have lived here their whole lives," she paused, trying to find the words. "As you might imagine, many of the members of our community take great pride that their ancestry goes all the way back to the very settling of this town. Understandably, they feel a certain ownership."

"I've noticed."

"Have you?" Aubry's eyebrows arched up, a slight smile touching at the sides of her paper-thin mouth. "Now I would never intrude on your hobbies. I just wanted to remind you that some people in this town care passionately about their little plot of land. Trespassing can bring out the worst in people."

"I know. I've already offended Mrs. Stelton for supposedly stealing her cemetery tour highlights," he said.

"Never mind Mrs. Stelton. All I'm saying is, just because something can be discovered doesn't mean that it necessarily should be."

"But what's wrong with uncovering the truth?"

Aubry smiled, patting his knee. "Oh, nothing, I suppose. But it doesn't mean everyone will thank you for it. Now you get a good night's rest, dear. Don't stay up too late."

Alone again, Edgar worked his grandmother's odd advice around in his head as he dipped the quill into the ink and let the ink curl onto the parchment once more.

Chapter 19

The house was silent.

From downstairs, the savory aroma of bacon and eggs crept through Edgar's bedroom door. There would be toast and freshly-squeezed orange juice, too. His grandmother always fixed a delicious Sunday breakfast for him before she left for church.

Edgar kicked the covers away as the smell brought him to life. "Ophelia Goodwicke," he grinned as memories of the previous night raced in. Sweeping fingers through his long, matted hair, he slid out of bed and took a glance out the window. This was it! Hopefully by evening's end they'd be finding out exactly what happened when the buttons were pushed together.

His spirits plummeted, however, as he read a text message from Shelby. "Been grounded," he repeated. He rubbed his eyes hard, causing brief fireworks to dance behind his eyelids. This was a disaster.

Edgar grabbed his robe and shuffled out into the hall. Would it be wrong for him and Corinthian to go ahead without Shelby and find out what was under that marker? What could she have done to get herself grounded anyway?

He'd just reached the bottom step of the staircase when Bach's *Toccata and Fugue in D Minor* piped from his cell phone. The number was unfamiliar.

"Hello, this is Edgar Wilde Tours."

"*Ahem,* yes, I'd like to schedule one of your creepy cemetery tour thingies. Dead bodies, right? And ghosts – can you arrange some ghosties to show up? But not those stupid orbs, though. I want the real deal."

"Shelby! How the hell could you get yourself grounded? Do you realize we can't go back out to the cemetery marker now? What did you do?"

"Mrs. Stelton happened. She raised a big stink about us being at the cemetery yesterday. Mom was mortified. Gave me hell when I got home. I'm locked in my fucking room."

"She locked you in?"

"I'm being melodramatic, stupid," she laughed. "But I might as well be a prisoner. Her office is downstairs and she's always working, so there's no sneaking by."

"Mrs. Stelton!" Edgar cursed. That woman was a gargantuan thorn in his side. He sat down to his eggs and bacon and braced himself. "So how long?"

"A week, but that'll go by in no time, right? In the meantime, I had an idea. We don't want to be seen in the cemetery when we go back to the marker, right? So, what if we ever-so-innocently try doing it during one of your next cemetery tours?"

Edgar put down his fork as his hopes plummeted further. "A whole week?"

"It'll go by in no time. Now listen, we'll just take your normal route, which you said goes by the marker. It'll just be a few flashlights in the dark, right? It'll look just like a tour. No one will be the wiser."

Edgar dabbled with his egg yolks, making them run slowly across the plate. A whole week! What a disaster.

"Just let me know when you're ready – after my sentence is up, of course," Shelby said. "I'll find a way to be there."

"Yeah, okay."

"You don't sound convinced. You're not going without me, are you?"

"Um, no. Of course not."

"Because I hear hesitation in your voice."

"No, we'll wait. Sure. It's just a week, and it's not your fault anyway."

"Now listen to me, Edgar Wilde, and listen carefully. If you go without me I am going to make your life intolerable. Are we clear?"

Edgar felt a shiver run through him. "I think I understand perfectly."

"Great!" Shelby lilted. "See you in a week!"

A creaking floorboard in the next room startled the fork right out of Edgar's hand. He barely had time to end the call before his grandmother strolled in.

"Good morning, Edgar!"

"Morning, Grandma," Edgar said, retrieving his fork from under his chair. "I didn't know you were still here. Aren't you supposed to be in church?"

"I'm attending a late service this morning. I'll be leaving soon. Oh, my! It's so nice to sleep in on a Sunday, isn't it? A little early to be on the phone."

"I was talking to a friend from school who had some questions about ghosts and supernatural occurrences."

"On a Sunday morning?" she replied, giving him a sidelong glance.

"It's for a school project. Everyone knows I'm into that kind of stuff, so she gave me a call."

"*She?* Oh, that's lovely," Aubry beamed. "Just don't scare her away with any of your antics."

Chapter 20

Smoky tendrils hung like cobwebs in the stale, dark air.

The St. Edmund Cemetery Administration Building storage room was really just a dank cellar filled with piles of records and other forgotten files. And thanks to the poor preservation efforts through the years it was all in a perpetual state of mildew and decay. If someone wanted the past to die there were few better places than this.

Corinthian inhaled again from his pipe, releasing more curls of pungent tobacco smoke into the thick air. In his other hand was a worn piece of paper. He'd found it inserted between two pages of the same ledger he'd shown Edgar and Shelby the night before.

As Corinthian brought the page close to the light, the faded words and symbols shadowed to life. Some he knew; others were maddeningly unfamiliar. There were references to common herbs, along with a scattering of alchemical jottings.

One edge of the sheet was rougher; it had clearly been torn from a book.

"Little page, where are all your brethren?" Corinthian took a quick swig of scotch. Smacking his lips, he pulled out the death ledger and turned to the fold where he'd found the loose sheet. There she was — the mysterious name *Ophelia Goodwicke* — brazenly scrawled over the erased name *Barnes Fullman*. Why had the mysterious little sheet been tucked there, of all places? It couldn't be coincidence. Somebody was trying to tell him something.

Ophelia, you witch. Who the hell are you anyway?

The tobacco crackled madly to life as he took another deep draw from his pipe. Perhaps tonight that saucy seductress would deign to reveal her goods to him, and his little page would finally speak its secrets.

"Time for you to lift your skirt and show us what you've got hiding under there," he grinned as he brought the bottle to his mouth.

Chapter 21

April 23, 1724. St. Edmund Island, Massachusetts.

The pews were empty. The rafters, silent.

They were all gone.

Reverend Allen's fingers finally unknotted. He looked down at the wooden floor, his eyes blurred with tears.

"A word?"

The reverend turned as Mayor Fullman's own daughter, Margharet, approached him from out of the shadows.

"Margharet, you haven't gone with the others."

"God save them. They know not –" The sudden wave of tears choked her voice back.

"Dear girl. I know this is hard. Your father's voice can be most convincing."

"Yet here you stand, reverend," she brought a handkerchief to her eyes as she moved closer. "His poison touches you not. You see him for what he be."

"Yet I did nothing."

"But what might you have done?" she said. Her eyes — a brilliant blue — shimmered through her tears.

"I don't know. I –" His thought was cut short by a movement to his left. "Old Lady Wallace!" She looked even older than he remembered.

"You may still do something if your conscience plague you."

Bethany Wallace had never been involved with the church, nor the community. She was spoken of with

hushed respect, but also with trepidation. She supposedly walked with the Evil One. The reverend stared at
her warily.

"What mean you by such a statement? My conscience
is not your concern."

"Innocent ones will perish this night, yet still you
tarry. What good be you then, *reverend?*"

Reverend Allen was shocked at the old woman's blunt
admonishment, the scorn with which she spoke his title.

"It is too late," he said. "What would you have me
do?"

"Protect this one," she pointed to Margharet. "Though
gifted in the ancient wisdoms, she must certainly be an
innocent in your eyes."

Reverend Allen felt his heart fall as he looked from
face to face.

"What? Lady Margharet, tell me truly. Serve you
the Evil One?"

Margharet looked deep into the reverend's eyes. "I
serve the cause of good, Reverend Allen. How could you
think otherwise of me? Do you question the wisdom of
the Moon less than the Sun?"

"My God," Reverend Allen crossed himself. It was as
much as a confession.

"It's true, my father fears me a witch," Margharet
said. "He found me in the care of Goody Wallace, without whom I certainly would have died. But the healing
remedies that saved my life are not evil! It is simply old
wisdom. But it matters not. He will not hear it. He is
set on my death. As I suppose you must be."

A convulsion brought her suddenly collapsing into
Reverend Allen's arms. He held her stiffly, trying not
to notice her voluptuousness and the alarming rush of
desire it caused deep within. He glanced at Goody Wallace, hoping she hadn't noticed.

"What is wrong with her?"

"Act now," the old woman whispered. "The babe may yet see tomorrow's dawn, but you must act!"

He froze. "What babe? Are you saying Margharet be with child?"

The old woman nodded.

"And the father?" He didn't know if the question stemmed from concern or jealousy.

"Hadley Williamson," Margharet said. "The tailor."

Hadley Williamson. A strapping lad, and a decent one, too. Allen shut his eyes, willing the inner conflict to abate. These were mortal matters. Yet the question of what his life might have been had he never taken the vows shook him to the foundation.

"You're a good man. Help find a path for this new soul."

The reverend stared hard at her. "Speak plainly. Is she requesting sanctuary of me?"

"I ask you to deliver both mother and child, in whatever way you be able. Deliver them from her vile father, and from this misguided village as well."

"Deliver them?" He reeled at the thought of what that meant. He would be helping an admitted witch and her illegitimate offspring escape the cleansing flame. But even he doubted the community was acting as God's instrument this night. And despite all he'd heard, in his heart he did believe Margharet was an innocent.

"Aye," the old woman replied. "By the love you bear her, you shall be their savior."

His Adam's apple rose and fell violently as he swallowed. Perhaps he'd been enchanted long ago and tonight the Devil was having his final laugh. For Reverend Allen loved the girl, and there was nothing to be done for it. How did the old woman know?

"Aye. So be it. Come then," he took the very pregnant Margharet gently by the arm and escorted her down into the church cellar. "I'll arrange transport to the mainland for you all, but you can bring nothing with you."

"I must stay here, Reverend Allen," the old woman said calmly as she looked down at them. "Margharet must never return to this place, nor her child. She must find her way to anonymity, and be content in her life. You'll make sure of that."

Reverend Allen took one last look at this mysterious old woman who followed not the ways of God yet somehow seemed His instrument in this moment. He closed the cellar door.

Chapter 22

Present Day. St. Edmund, Massachusetts.

Edgar stared out his bedroom window.

Beyond the skeletal trees and snow-capped houses he could see the cemetery's protruding gravestones, rising out of the white drifts like crooked teeth.

The town's first snow of the year had begun the same morning Edgar and Shelby had made their plan to return to the cemetery. Over the next few days it only intensified, becoming one of the worst snowstorms St. Edmund Island had seen in decades.

"You're fortunate to be in Florida, Dade. I'm going crazy stuck in this room when the secret of the Ophelia Goodwicke marker is waiting for me only a few blocks away."

The book dealer was finishing off a very messy Reuben onscreen, accumulating bits of corned beef and sauerkraut in his goatee and on his Hawaiian shirt.

"I hear that from tourists all the time," Dade chomped away. "You should come try the heat, man. I guarantee you'll be wishing for snow then. I'd move to New England in a heartbeat if I could. That's where all the best old books are anyway. So you're sure about that button?"

"Absolutely. I saw Shelby push it in." Edgar watched in fascination as Dade continued to ignore the need of a napkin.

"It's a cool story, man. Never heard of anything like it. 1732, huh? Well you know that can't be right. That's at least 150 years too early for the manufactured metal stuff, but I'm sure you already thought of that. You've got a real mystery there. Wish I could help. Not to change the subject, but have you found out anything about that book?"

"I checked at The Owl again, but no luck. If you could give me more details maybe I could get a lead on it."

"Man, you know what I know. I've got to track this thing down," Dade sounded even more despondent than before. "I'd be able to start closing the bookstore on Saturdays for the money my client has offered. Ever see *The Ninth Gate* with Johnny Depp? It's starting to feel like that. This guy is really on my back."

"Who exactly is this crazy client?" Edgar asked. "How can any book concerning herbs and spells be worth that much? I mean they don't actually work, right?"

Dade's eyes bulged wide at Edgar from across seven states.

"Do the spells in the book work, you mean? It's magic spells, Edgar! Of course they don't work. Some collectors need every freakin' thing that exists on a particular subject. I figure he's just a nut job. But the important thing is, he's got the green. You get that book and you will be well-compensated, my friend."

Dade gave him a quick wave and pessimistic smile as he hung up. Edgar turned and gazed out over the placid expanse of snow. The drifts were high enough to jump right into from his second-story window.

Before he could contemplate the risks of such a daring exploit, however, *Toccata and Fugue* piped from his cellphone. Edgar snatched it up.

"Dear boy, do forgive me, but I just got so bored. Would you care to see something amazing?"

Chapter 23

The steam plumed out of the coffee cup lids, little smoke-stacks in tiny wrinkled hands.

Cora stood deep in snow, having trudged from her house all the way to Gertrude's shop. Her legs were throbbing from the half-mile trek; she sorely regretted ever letting Gertrude convince her to get out of bed, let alone walk all the way to her store. Gertrude hadn't spoken to Cora in days, ever since she'd found out about the cemetery confrontation. And now she wanted coffee brought to her?

Gertrude had shoveled the sidewalk section in front of her store early that morning, leaving behind a perfect, exposed square of pavement. Cora made a disgusting sound with her mouth as she intentionally shuffled through the bare patch on her way into the store.

"See you finally got around to getting me my coffee." Gertrude noted with thinly-veiled contempt the piles of melty slush that followed Cora in.

"I'm cold as a witch's tit," Cora said.

"Is that supposed to be funny?" Gertrude gave Cora a seething glance as she took her coffee and sat back down. "So you had to confront Harknell and the others out there, did you? You might as well have waved a red flag."

"What did you expect me to do?" Cora fumed. "The Goodwicke marker is one of my tour highlights! I told you, I've got it in my brochure!"

"Cora, you've apparently forgotten why the Historical Society tasked you with doing those tours in the first place."

Cora brushed down her coat and looked off to the left, searching the walls for something important to focus on. "I remember," she whispered. "To protect the secret."

"*The secret,*" Gertrude echoed, downing her coffee. "Now I don't know what you could have possibly been thinking by making a scene out there, but I can assure you it has not helped."

Suddenly Gertrude's cellphone rang. She pressed it to her ear and remained silent as she listened to what the caller had to say.

"How should I know that?" she finally replied, her cheeks flushed. "I haven't left my shop all morning. What? Well I'm sure I didn't even know Harknell had a key!"

The key. Cora closed her eyes, mortified. She'd slipped a key to the Historical Society House to Corinthian many years back, when he'd needed to do some cemetery research.

"I see. And you know for sure he's in there right now," Gertrude continued, turning slowly to Cora.

Cora brushed fake mistletoe out of her face as she peered out the storefront window. She could see the top floor of the Historical Society House a few blocks away; God only knew what that man was into at that very moment. "Blast!" she whispered, then covered her mouth as she turned to see Gertrude staring at her.

"Yes, I know that's my job," Gertrude said evenly to the caller. "No, we'll take care of it. What? Oh, yes, she's right here."

Cora's eyes widened. Why would the caller want to talk to her? The blood drained from her as she took the

70

phone from Gertrude.

"Hello?" Her voice sounded shaky. It didn't help that Gertrude was watching her. On the other end was silence.

"H... Hello?" she repeated.

More silence.

Finally she glanced at the screen, only to discover that whoever it was had already ended the call.

"You are going to pay for that, Gertrude!"

"So you gave Corinthian the key, did you?"

"That was a long time ago!" Cora yelled. "How'm I supposed to remember every key that passes through my hands?"

"Sitting on a pile of keys, are you? You're slipping in your old age, Cora. Thanks to you, I've got to lock up the store while we go traipse up to the Historical Society House, and that's costing me valuable customers."

"It's just a dang key," Cora fumed as they donned coats and scarves. "Besides, I don't exactly see any customers fighting to get in here."

"We're sworn to keep our secrets. Now, thanks to you, Harknell is messing about in the Historical Society House. Who knows what he'll find?"

"But there's nothing! You should know that better than anyone. He ain't going to find what ain't there."

"There's the map, Cora. Right out there in the open, too. Curse you and your key! Now I can't even enjoy my coffee."

"Just a dang key," Cora mumbled as they made their way out into the snow.

Chapter 24

Edgar was out the door before Corinthian even had a chance to finish the question.

The St. Edmund Historical Society House was a nut he'd been trying to crack for a very long time. He practically salivated over the historical documents that lay within, but his requests for access had always been denied. How Corinthian had gotten in was a mystery, but he wasn't about to turn down such a rare opportunity.

As he stepped out into the snow, his head turned briefly in the direction of the cemetery. Ah, well. They wouldn't be able to do anything anyway; the snow would make lifting the marker difficult, and it would be too easy for the three of them to be spotted. In the meantime, exploring the bowels of the Historical Society House was a welcome diversion!

When Edgar entered the ornately-painted Colonial structure a few minutes later he'd hoped for a blast of welcoming warmth. Instead, he was greeted by an icy chill he could swear was even colder than the outside air.

"Oh my God, Corinthian! Where's the heat?"

"Sorry lad." Corinthian was wearing a fuzzy, black toboggan with a little ball on top. "The building has been closed since the snow fell. No one's been in here for quite a while. But it allows for a bit of privacy."

"Only the dead would be caught in this icebox," Edgar mumbled as they reached the main archive room.

"Let's hope we're not," Corinthian said as he un-locked the door, then smiled at Edgar. "Caught, I mean. Now, here's what I wanted to show you –"

As the heavy, oak door gave way, Edgar's heart started to pound. It was a breathtaking pile of local history spread out before them. Dusty, poorly-rendered oil portraits of past Society officers hung on almost every wall, while at the far end a huge old map of St. Edmund Island stretched from one end to the other. And positioned randomly throughout the room were ceiling-high bookshelves, all packed to capacity with assorted volumes, folders and boxes. It was a history buff's dream, but was clearly not being properly tended to.

"Look at this mess! Who runs this place?"

"Come on, let's not dawdle," Corinthian said. "There'll be plenty of time later to drop something in the suggestion box if the room doesn't meet with your approval."

Each quickly grabbed a stack of historic records and sat down on opposite sides of a long oak table.

Edgar's numb fingers dug into the pile in front of him. Three pages of World War II-era military documents rested atop a copy of a local gas-rationing plan, circa 1975. Under that was a thin book on Masonic burial rites (Edgar resisted the urge to pocket that one), and below that, a copy of a 1963 newspaper clipping reporting the assassination of John F. Kennedy. There was no telling what would be next. It was complete and utter chaos. Edgar shook his head as he lifted each page and lay it carefully to the side; the incredible lack of organization seemed almost intentional.

But that would be ridiculous.

He was trudging through some water-damaged papers having to do with property taxes when Corinthian suddenly broke through the silence.

"And I, of ladies most deject and wretched..."

"Corinthian, what the hell?"

"Shakespeare, my boy. I was just pondering over who our mysterious Ophelia Goodwicke might be. A pseudonym maybe? Anagram? We must set our minds to puzzling out why those were the two particular words chosen."

"And Ophelia is from *Hamlet,* right? Let's see – I remember that Ophelia committed suicide."

"No, she didn't, actually," Corinthian corrected. "In truth she fell from a willow tree and drowned. That could be relevant; the willow tree is a symbol of regret common to many old gravestones. And I'm sure you remember that it happens to be on Ophelia's marker as well."

"But what about the last name?" Edgar replied. "I don't know any literary reference to *Goodwicke.*"

"That part eludes me," Corinthian stood up to stretch his legs. "I'm quite certain there are no families with that name on this island, nor are there any other Goodwickes in the cemetery."

Corinthian turned around to find himself in front of the large map. He shifted his bifocals to bring the details into sharp focus.

"What an excellent old map," he said as he read the credit at the bottom right. "This is the original, too. A fellow named Arnot was the artist. French descent, I suppose. Dated 1885. I must say, I've never seen this one before. I wonder why I haven't run into a copy in all my years –"

Edgar felt his cellphone vibrate. It was Shelby.

"Edgar, are you in the Historical Society House?"

"Hey Shelby," Edgar clamped the cellphone against his ear. "How did you know? We're in the archive room right now doing some research."

"Edgar, my mom was just on the phone talking to someone about tracks in the snow leading to the Historical Society House, and how it must be Corinthian. She told whoever was on the other end to take care of it. I'm not sure what that means, but I think you guys really need to get out of there."

Weird. Why would Shelby's mom care about that?

"Thanks for the heads up, Shelby. We'll start packing up now."

"So, did you find anything? I can't believe you didn't even call me!"

"Shelby, we're not in the cemetery. It's just some boring research. I actually didn't think you'd be interested."

"Is that so? I'll have you know I've been doing my own research while you've been out doing stuff without me," Shelby huffed. "And I'm not going to tell you what I've found, either."

"I suppose we'll just have to manage without that vital piece of information from *Teen Vogue*," Edgar replied dryly. "I'll call you later."

"Promise."

"Good bye, Shelby!" he yelled, and hung up.

"Our dear flower," Corinthian said.

"We probably should have invited her along," Edgar sighed. "I never would have guessed she'd be so into this."

"So what did your *acquaintance* have to say?" Corinthian asked, his eyes glued to a section of the old map. Edgar noted his friend's sarcasm.

"We're not dating, Corinthian!"

"Go on, go on," Corinthian shot Edgar a playful jab of a glance. "What news from our little *Mata Hari?*"

"She said someone's on their way to check out who's in the building."

Corinthian turned, staring coldly at Edgar over his bifocals.

"Now how did she know that?"

"Somebody saw tracks in the snow. Corinthian, what's up with the map? Want me to take some pictures?"

"No, let's leave it in peace for now. It has said enough for one day." He paused there, gently patting the map, which was protected behind a pane of thick glass. He then gave Edgar a sheepish grin and nodded for them to go.

Edgar wondered sometimes whether his friend wasn't just a little bit senile.

Chapter 25

"Making good use of your time? I thought 'grounded' also meant no calls."

Shelby turned to see her mother standing at the bedroom door.

"Mom, I didn't see you there."

"Well?" Stephanie continued to stare at the cellphone in Shelby's hand.

"Edgar. It was Edgar."

"I see. The Wilde boy," Stephanie said. "You do realize he's a big part of the reason you are grounded right now. So, anything I might be interested in?"

"He just called to see how I was doing," Shelby lied.

Stephanie sat down on the bed and ran a finger along one of the seams of the bunched comforter. Shelby's brow furrowed in irritation as her mother remained accusingly silent. They could do a silent fight like this for hours.

"Mom, I said I was sorry about the cemetery thing. I can't help it if a friend calls me."

"*A friend?* Is that what he is now?" Stephanie stood and sweetly wrapped her arms around her daughter. "Shelby, I know how easy it can be to get caught up in things if you don't have your guard up. Edgar Wilde is the last person you want as a friend."

Shelby pulled away and turned to the window, her arms crossed. "Honestly, I'm not sure why you even care, and I really wish you didn't."

"Shelby, dear, imagine your friends seeing you in that cemetery, standing there with that boy — and Corinthian Harknell of all people!" Stephanie raised a hand to her forehead dramatically. "I just can't bear the thought of you getting drawn into such a macabre group of misfits. It is so, so easy for one's reputation to be irreparably tarnished by the company one keeps."

"Mom, I..."

"I love you dearly, sweetheart," Stephanie consoled. "From now on I must insist you leave the Wilde boy alone. He's got a way of finding trouble. Poor boy — no proper role model, I suppose. I know you don't see it right now, but believe me, you'll thank me later for this. You don't need someone like that in your life. He's comes from the wrong side of town."

"He lives three streets over!"

"You know what I mean, dear. Now let's consider this topic closed and have no more fuss. Oh, you do remember the soiree we're going to next week? I have a delightful dress picked out for you — a low-cut blue number to highlight your hair. You're still a size six, aren't you? You know how winter can do a number on your figure if you're not careful. I can't wait until my friends see you in that dress! It will be like a coming-out party for you. What about shoes? I was thinking black pumps. And I think that boy Robert will be there — you remember him don't you? Now he's a fine catch. I don't mind telling you that if I was a few years younger –!"

Shelby could feel tears beginning to smolder down her cheeks. She watched the window without turning until the reflection of her mom finally left the room. Locking the door, she grabbed a high school yearbook off the shelf and flopped onto the bed.

Edgar's photo was halfway down page 62. He looked even paler in the photo. Strands of long, black hair hung rebelliously over his face, like he'd been caught in a storm out at sea. And there were his dark green eyes –

Closing the book, she rolled over and considered calling one of her friends, then thought better of it. They would never be receptive to any thoughts having to do with Edgar Wilde.

Chapter 26

The key — and that deceitful Corinthian.

Cora had buried the memory of it all. It hadn't even occurred to her that he'd ever think to use it again. She should have known better.

She covered her mouth as unwanted memories came back — of his lips on hers, his wit charming her, breaking through her defenses one magnificent compliment after another. It had only been a few encounters, and years ago at that. Still, her cheeks flushed at the memory.

She glanced up at Gertrude, mortified. Her friend would never let her hear the end of it if she found out.

The St. Edmund Historical Society House stood silent as they turned the corner. Leading to it, two deep sets of boot prints marked their way through the snow. Cora and Gertrude quickly noted a second trail of prints leading out of the building and around the corner as well.

"They've gone," Cora said.

"Appears so," Gertrude replied tersely.

They glanced at the door.

"Should we go in?" Cora whispered, shivering uncontrollably now they had stopped.

"To check things out anyway, I suppose," Gertrude looked towards the sky, but didn't move. "No heat inside, though. And it's obvious they've gone anyway."

"Done what we could, you know," Cora said. "Trudged all the way out here and all."

"Checked it out," Gertrude agreed. "The devils took off already."

"And they couldn't have found nothin' anyway."

"What's to find?" Gertrude said. "Except tracks in the snow."

Cora and Gertrude didn't often agree on much, so the two old women found it portentous that they'd so sagely come to the same conclusion.

Without saying another word, they turned and followed their own tracks all the way back to the store.

Chapter 27

"Edgar, hi! Look at you two, all frozen!"

Sarah the Barista looped a strand of auburn hair back behind a cherubic ear as Edgar and Corinthian entered the coffee shop.

"Sarah, don't you look especially fetching on this cold winter's day," Corinthian replied as he leaned over the counter. "The chill has certainly added some rose to your cheek."

Edgar stared at his friend in slightly sickened awe. Corinthian was never at a loss for charming banter.

"Thank you, Mr. Harknell!" Sarah's complexion deepened into merlot.

"And what delightful roast of the day would you recommend to two snow-weary journeyers who have plowed their way through the glacial plains to finally arrive on your welcoming doorstep?"

Sarah was in full swoon now, completely overwhelmed by the amorous bombardment. She failed miserably to find things for her hands to do as she tried to remember the day's special.

"The Fall River Vienna is remarkable for its, um, refreshing boldness and its spicy undertones. We brew our beans fresh every day, um, over in Fall River."

"How could I forget," Corinthian replied. "Your Fall River roasts are legendary. I do believe that's where Lizzie Borden let the ax fall on her family, is it not?

The Vienna sounds most welcome. Please, brew me as you will."

Sarah's sudden maniacal giggling at Corinthian's banter made Edgar jerk back. He couldn't stop a nervous laugh from escaping his own mouth as she turned to him.

"And you, Edgar? How may I *brew you* today?"

Edgar's mouth opened but nothing came out. Corinthian's reference to the infamous Lizzie Borden had him suddenly visualizing the many ways Sarah the Barista might finally lose it and kill those she'd taken a liking to.

"I assure you Edgar is in sore need of some brewing. Why I can tell you –"

"Sumatra!" Edgar yelled. "And cinnamon! Shaved fresh. And Fall River beans. And – cinnamon!"

Sarah gave Edgar a radiant smile as she spun to prepare their order. Corinthian and Edgar crossed to a round drum of a table in the corner. Once seated, Edgar buried his face in his hands. Corinthian reached over and gave him a consoling pat on the back.

"She seems delightful! My God, but I do believe you have two women fighting over you. Good show! And you almost managed to be coherent back there as well."

"Shut up."

"You'll eventually have to choose, you know. It's a burden being a handsome rogue, believe you me."

"Moving on now –"

"Alas, will you leave Shelby by the wayside as you tarry with this new plump morsel?"

Edgar made a strangled noise. "Shelby? Corinthian, what are you talking about?"

"There's no mistaking the delicious spark between you and Miss Emerson. I figured it was only a matter of time."

The coffees arrived at that moment. Sarah the Barista was a blur as she came and went.

"Oh, dear. Do you think she overheard? Another lover spurned, I suppose."

Edgar moaned. "I really don't know what this fascination is with Shelby being a match for me. She's just an acquaintance."

"An acquaintance. Yes, you said that before."

"For some reason she's curious about Fullman and the cemetery. It doesn't mean anything else!" Edgar brought the cup to his mouth with both hands and took a hot sip. "I mean, I'm not saying she's not attractive. She does this funny thing with her hair, for instance – pulls it back behind her ears when she's trying to focus."

"*Ears?*" Corinthian mocked. "*Ears,* you say? My God, could Cupid have aimed any better?"

"I was just pointing it out! That doesn't mean I'm actually interested in her."

"Ah, my poor young friend. Strapped to the mast as the siren's song calls."

"So how is your Sumatra with cinnamon?" Sarah the Barista stood over her two customers, a slight giggle still quivering her voice.

"Good cinnamon," Edgar mumbled as the hot coffee scalded the roof of his mouth. It was becoming a familiar experience.

"My dear, it's as if each bean has been touched by your radiant warmth, by your loving touch," Corinthian waxed.

"Good cinnamon!" Edgar yelled at Corinthian.

Sarah smiled and — Edgar could have sworn — curtsied slightly before darting back to the counter.

Corinthian eyed him mischievously. "You want to know about the sketch of the island, then. The one I couldn't be pried away from."

Edgar rolled his burnt tongue in his mouth. "You saw something important?"

Corinthian thumbed the lid of his coffee. "There was a word on it. A name, actually. I'm not sure what it was doing there, but it may eventually have some relevance to our quest."

"Yes?"

"*Himmelhaus.*"

"House of God," Edgar whispered, translating the German. "A church, then?"

"I don't think so. The word wasn't next to any structure. Anyway, I'm quite familiar with all the churches this town has seen. No, this was different. Each letter of the word was located at a different street intersection, and they were much smaller than the other typestyles on the map as well. If you weren't looking for it you might just see an *m* and not even think to look over one intersection to see the next letter. It seems like the word was intentionally hidden in plain sight, but I can't imagine why."

"Maybe it was the name of a special street?"

Corinthian pondered his coffee. "A street named *House of God.* The road to Heaven is paved with good intentions, but I don't think this particular road leads there. No, it's something else. A mystery for now, I suppose."

"Unfortunately, that's about the only interesting thing we found at the Historical Society," Edgar sighed. "Otherwise, the visit was something of a bust."

"But you did have a jolly time, didn't you?" Corinthian smiled. "And see! Have you ever had a more delicious cup of coffee in your life?"

They both looked over to see Sarah the Barista at the counter, ogling Edgar intensely. She curtsied again, and an unrestrained giggle echoed across the room.

Edgar instinctively covered his neck as they grabbed their cups and left the store.

Chapter 28

The snowstorm had done a number on Aubry's backyard garden.

The annuals and perennials were beyond help. And the rows of miniature conifers had been bent low by the weight of the snow, but they might possibly be salvaged. Only the curling ivy that embraced the edges of the garden had held its ground successfully.

Clever ivy.

"I suppose we'll have to see what we can do," she whispered, wiping her hands on a towel.

A nudge against her leg brought Aubry down to give a quick bit of affection to Anise, the neighbors' ever-curious Russian Blue. The cat had years ago annexed all of Aubry's property as an extension of its own, and Aubry had grown quite fond of the silent companionship as she tended to her garden and sipped tea on warm summer days.

"What do you make of all this, *Little Star?* Are the mice back out yet?" Anise purred gratefully against her delicate fingers. "Poor dear. I suppose we'll have to help you out a bit until they return."

A few minutes later, Anise was settled into devouring the meal of fresh North Atlantic salmon Aubry had brought out for her. *There's no gratitude like the joyful silence that comes from a cat no longer hungry.*

"Ummm... excuse me?"

Aubry glanced up to see a blonde girl smiling at her.

"Well, isn't this an unexpected surprise. My dear, for a moment I mistook you for your mother. It's been a while, Shelby. How lovely to see you. How is Stephanie, by the way?"

"Hello, Mrs. Wilde. Mom's fine. She's been pretty stressed, but it's okay. I mean, that's sort of how she is anyway."

"I imagine she's very busy these days," Aubry replied as she brought Anise up to hang on a shoulder. "The snowstorm has surely had an impact on the tourism."

"Tourism?" Shelby looked down at her feet, now settled in a muddy patch of ground. She shifted her feet a bit and felt a shoe start to pull away from her heel.

"Not tourism, then?" Aubry asked casually. "I can't imagine what could be distracting her. Oh, dear – look at your shoes."

"No, I'm sure it's the tourism," Shelby worked to gracefully exit the muddy trap. "I actually don't pay much attention to what mom is into."

"Here to see Edgar then, I suppose?

Shelby nodded.

"Well go on in, dear. He's up in his room, into all sorts of mischief, no doubt." Aubry gave Shelby the barest flitter of a wink and glanced toward the back door of the house. "Watch the screen door, dear — there's a hinge loose. And would you please be so kind as to take your shoes off in the entryway?"

"Of course. Thank you, Mrs. Wilde."

Aubry listened patiently as the back door closed with a familiar squeak and click, then took a deep breath and contemplated the remains of her garden. Sensing a change in her mood, Anise jumped down and scurried underneath a nearby chair to observe whatever might come next.

Chapter 29

Upstairs, Edgar's room was all roads, houses and landmarks.

Edgar had pulled out every map he had of the town; they were all open now and strewn across the room. He sat in his chair, legs crossed, fingers interlocked, looking for all the world like some sort of Buddhist monk deep in meditation.

Himmelhaus.

None of his maps hinted at any weird lettering at intersections like the one Corinthian saw at the Historical Society House. It didn't make sense. Why hadn't Corinthian pointed the odd name out to him while they were actually there so he could see it for himself? He regretted not taking some decent photos of that map when he had the chance. It hadn't occurred to him it might be the only copy.

A knock on the door startled Edgar out of his pondering. He looked up, completely disoriented.

"Yes, grandma?"

"No, it's just me," Shelby's head peeked through the door. Her eyes widened at Edgar's room, the maps piled high.

"Holy crap, Edgar! Having a little trouble finding your way around St. Edmund? They have GPS now, you know."

"Shelby! What are you doing here?"

Shelby plopped carelessly onto the assorted maps that covered the bed. Edgar winced as she reclined, apparently oblivious to the resulting damage she was causing. He started to say something, but held his breath instead.

She was in his room.

It didn't help that Shelby was looking alarmingly cute. She wore a blue knit cap with little dangly puff balls, setting off curly strands of blonde hair as they spiraled out from underneath. And her form-fitting black wool jacket only accentuated the curve of her jean-clad legs, which seemed to go on forever but instead finally ended with a pair of fuzzy blue socks. Edgar glanced down nervously and was mortified to realize he hadn't dressed yet — he was still wearing faded, pin-striped pajamas.

"I just needed to get out of the house, and I thought, why not visit my favorite weirdo? That okay?"

"Yeah – sure."

Edgar watched with trepidation as her eyes scanned the room. A nightmare was already forming in his head of Shelby gossiping to her idiotic school friends about where Edgar lived, and what his room looked like. Why couldn't she have texted or something before deciding to stop by?

"This place is amazing," Shelby finally whispered. "Edgar, I don't believe you live here! Look at all the books! And the cool antiques. Is that a real microscope? Ooh, it's an old one, too! Hey, I was thinking – want to go get some coffee? You look like you could use a break from whatever it is you're doing up here."

Edgar hated himself as an audible sigh of relief escaped his lips – as if he really cared what she thought! Still, he had to admit that her enthusiasm was alarmingly intoxicating. "Sure. Why not?" He hoped he sounded like he didn't care.

"Great! Umm – you will put on some clothes, won't you?"

A few minutes later, Shelby and Edgar — now attired in his normal black gothic finery — left the house. Outside, Aubry was on the ground, gently tilling the soil. Around her, the miniature conifers were now branching tall and radiant green in the sunlight, and the first flower buds of the year were already peeking out from the soil.

Shelby stopped in her tracks, certain that she'd seen a small wasteland of a garden just a few minutes before.

"These little souls do hang on for dear life, don't they?" Aubry sang as they walked by. "You two have a wonderful walk now."

Chapter 30

"You still need us, Mr. Corinthian?"

As always, the two boys had done a good job helping Corinthian prepare the newest burial spot. Strong arms for cheap wages — teenagers could always be counted on.

"Take off, lads. See you here bright and early tomorrow."

Corinthian turned back to the hollow pit they'd spent the day creating. Gathering gloves and shovels, he tipped his hat to the vacant ground and walked to the storage shed.

"Brooks gone, huh?"

Cora Stelton stood at the door of the shed. "Got to admit, I thought he'd last longer against the cancer. He was an ox of a man."

"Indeed," Corinthian mumbled as he hung up the shovels. "Small things sometimes bring down great men."

"Now you'll be sharing your barstool with that Wilde boy instead, of all things. So, what'd you find, Harknell? I didn't take you for a trespasser. Left things all out of order, too."

"Trespasser?" Corinthian smiled but didn't turn to look at her. "My good woman, I had a key, as you'll no doubt recall. Well earned, too. Yet even though *your* doors opened for a brief spell, the Historical Society's remained sealed to me? As curator of our town's deceased, I would think I'd have access to every nook and cranny. I can't imagine why you'd deny me access to those records. I certainly meant no harm."

Cora stood directly behind Corinthian, clenched fists pressed deep into her ample sides. His biting diatribe had found its target.

"If I'd known your true intent, I'd have made sure no door ever opened for you — including mine!"

"Oh dear. That would have been a tragedy."

"What have you roped that boy into helping you find, Harknell? Cause there's nothing needs finding in this town!"

"Edgar? Oh, he had a school project. Cemetery stuff. The boy does enjoy his history, you know."

"I advise you to leave things alone!" Cora spat. "The officers of the St. Edmund Historical Society are sworn to protect –"

Even as the words left her mouth she knew she'd said too much. Corinthian spun around and gave her a toothy grin.

"So you've even taken an oath, then. It must be something shockingly important that you and your friends are protecting. Wouldn't you like to share your little secret with a dear old friend? We were quite intimate, you and I, once upon a time. Or is it possible you've forgotten?"

Cora backed up, feeling her way toward the shed door. In all the years she'd known him she'd never felt scared in Corinthian's presence. Until this moment.

"You're in my debt, Corinthian. Don't forget I did you a good deed all those years ago. Got you this job when you were down, because of what we had together. The least you can do is show some respect and keep your nose out of things."

"Are you collecting on your debt, then, Cora? Is that your price — my receding curiosity? Well I don't accept your terms, madam!" At this, Corinthian broke into an erratic little jig. "You've held that little favor over my head so many years I'd actually come to dread the day you chose to cash in. Instead, here you've just lit a magnificent fire under me! Well played, madam."

"What on earth do you mean?" Cora asked sharply.

"It must indeed be an incredible thing you are hiding, Cora. You've all but confirmed it. And aren't you a dear for giving me such hope! Now I know for certain there's truth to the whispers."

Cora stood still, mouth agape. "You won't stop," she whispered.

Corinthian leaned in so that his mouth was right beside her ear.

"No, madam, I most certainly will not. You've treated me bitterly these long years, and held your damned, pathetic debt over my head like a *Sword of Damocles*. Now I think I'll have your head for a change. Madam, like it or not, I will have that Grimoire."

Chapter 31

"... And over there, I once watched a sailboat sink."

Shelby leaned into Edgar, pointing at the shimmering St. Edmund Bay. "Everyone got out. The whole family swam all the way over to the pier – including their dog! The boat's still under the water, right over there. Sometimes I think about salvaging it, and then I'd have a sailboat."

"You know how to sail?" Edgar watched the little blue balls of yarn on Shelby's cap dance as the cold breeze swept around them.

"No, but that's no problem," she said, working to bring some wild tangles of blonde under control by tucking them in her cap. "Wouldn't it be cool, Edgar? Just head out the bay and go wherever you want. I would so love that. Anyone can sail. I just need a few lessons."

"And the boat."

"And the boat," Shelby repeated. "Wouldn't you love to just sail away to somewhere completely new?"

Edgar stole a glance. Shelby's blue eyes sparkled madly in the sunlight as she beamed at him.

"Anywhere would be better than here," he said. "You may not have noticed, but I don't really fit in."

"Hmmm. Now that you mention it –"

Edgar shook his head. "It's not like a secret or anything. I've never really felt I belong here."

"I don't know," Shelby replied as they strolled back

up the street. "In a weird way you sort of *really* belong here. This town is pretty eccentric and historic when you think about it. Lots of mystery and secrets. I'd say that describes you as well."

"Sums me up, I suppose?"

"No, not nearly," Shelby gave Edgar's arm a quick, playful nudge. "But it's a start. I'll let you know when I come up with more."

"Um, let's get that coffee, shall we?" Edgar walked faster, flustered by Shelby's flirtatious play.

"Come on, then!" she replied, locking her arm through his before he could do anything. "I'm freezing!"

As Shelby pulled Edgar into the shops along the way, he noted bemused glances from some of the locals who knew him. His dignity was being thoroughly dashed against the rocks as Shelby tugged him by his coat sleeve toward various tourist traps, the likes of which he'd — until now — done well to avoid.

"Come on, Shelby –" he resisted, only to be pulled harder by his eager companion.

"You've got to see this!" she said as they entered a shop with a plastic lobster hanging over the door. "Have you ever been in here? Come on, check out what's in the back!"

Before he knew it, Edgar was standing in front of a plastic lobster the size of a couch. It was such a disarming, unexpected surprise that Edgar couldn't help bursting out in laughter.

"Isn't this insane?" Shelby said. "Come on, they take your picture with it, too!"

Chapter 32

As they entered The Magic Bean a few minutes later, Edgar and Shelby were still laughing at photos of the two of them sitting on the ridiculous giant lobster's claws.

"I've walked by that place hundreds of times," Edgar laughed. "I had no idea they had a lobster in there! Who came up with *that?*"

"Can I help you?"

Sarah the Barista stood at the counter, waiting patiently to take their order.

"Hey Sarah. Can I get a cinnamon latte?"

"Sure. You?" she looked neutrally at Shelby.

"Oh, something with caramel, I think."

"Caramel latte coming up."

Before they knew it, their drinks were on the counter and the change was in Edgar's hand. It was the single most efficient exchange he'd ever had with Sarah the Barista. The abruptness was incredibly awkward. Corinthian's annoying rant about romance from a few days ago came fluttering back into his mind, causing him to fume quietly.

As they grabbed their coffees and made their way out the door, Edgar stole a nervous look back. Surely he'd been imagining things. But it was as he'd feared; Sarah the Barista stood there, eyes focused jealously on Shelby. Edgar could only be thankful Corinthian wasn't around to witness this bizarre encounter.

He would certainly never hear the end of it.

Chapter 33

"Well, now. Isn't that a sight?"

Cora's breath frosted the glass as she watched Edgar and Shelby strolling down the opposite sidewalk, sipping coffees and laughing. "Looks like Stephanie's daughter has landed herself quite a prize. I can't wait to see the look on her face."

"Shut up!" Gertrude failed yet again to thread the eye of her needle. "Young love is not our concern. Your blunder with the key has cost us dearly. That fingerprint on the old map could only belong to Harknell. He was taunting us; he knew we'd see his dirty old print right there on the glass. He found it, Cora. Corinthian Harknell found the hidden word on the map. Fortunately, he doesn't know much else – yet. But we've got to be careful."

Cora paced about nervously, her arms crossed. Finally she burst out. "What could he want with the Grimoire anyway?"

Gertrude's eyes shot coldly over her bifocals. "The Grimoire? He couldn't possibly know about the book."

"It's true. It's what he's wrangled that Wilde boy to help him locate."

Gertrude returned to her threading, her hand jerky with irritation. "There's no way you could possibly know that, Cora dear. To know that, you'd had to have talked with the man. I'm sure that's impossible, what with your disastrous encounter at the cemetery just a few days ago."

Gertrude's hand stopped, mid-thread, as she watched Cora's eyes fall to the floor in shame.

"Dear God, you've gone and talked to him again," Gertrude rose from her chair, shaking her head in bewilderment. "Well, you're certainly a pickle in a jar now."

"I had to get the key from him, didn't I?" Cora flustered.

"So let's have the key then," Gertrude thrust an open hand out impatiently. "At least we'll have tied up one loose thread. That should allay Stephanie for a little while, anyway."

"Umm, I don't – that is, you see –" Cora replied evasively.

"Cora, you risked a great deal to get back that key. Now you did get it, didn't you?"

"He distracted me with his silken snake tongue!"

"What *snake tongue?* So, you exposed us all again and you didn't even get the key. Could you possibly be any more useless?"

"But the book – the Grimoire! He called it by name. I asked him to leave it alone, I really did! But he wouldn't hear of it. He's wicked hellbent to have it!"

Gertrude's wrinkled hands folded tightly.

"I don't know why he thinks the damned thing even exists," she whispered, more to herself than Cora. "It's just a legend. I wonder if he could really be close to finding it."

"He found *Himmelhaus,* and that's real enough. Just think, Gertrude – *the Grimoire!*"

"That would indeed be something," Gertrude could almost feel the pages between her fingers. "I don't mind telling you I've dreamt of it."

"*We* both have," Cora corrected.

"Of course."

Chapter 34

April 23, 1724. St. Edmund Island, Massachusetts.

"Reverend Allen!"

The reverend tugged at the worn, leather reins, bringing the horse and wagon to a stop. The twilight sky was fast turning toward nightfall, making the approaching figure difficult to make out. Reverend Allen felt panic take hold of his body. The horse sensed his mood, pulling angrily at the bit.

"Who approaches?"

"Hadley Williamson, reverend. I see you're in haste, but a word please?"

"Hadley!" Margharet's head rose from out of the wagon.

"Dear God!" Reverend Allen whispered. "Margharet, you must not be seen! Quickly now, or we are all forfeit!"

"What is this?" Hadley helped her down from the wagon. "I've been searching everywhere for you, but – be you leaving?"

"My love, you know well that father has roused the town into a frenzy. Goody Wallace enlisted the reverend to find a safe place for me until the storm has passed."

"Mean you Anne Wallace? The witch?" Hadley responded. "What's this to do with you? Why consort with such company?"

"Friends," Reverend Allen whispered loudly. "There is no time. While you tarry the village folk sharpen their daggers. We must away while we can! Mr. Williamson, forgive my impertinence but all is known to me; I will do everything I can to save your unborn child. You are welcomed to join us, but pray hurry!"

Hadley took Margharet violently by the arm. "Be you a witch as well?" he seethed.

"I am only a midwife, my love," she pulled back. "And I know some *physick*. It is all good and godly stuff. There is no evil in what I do!"

Reverend Allen knew the look in Hadley's eyes. He lowered himself quietly to the ground.

"You deceived me!" Hadley cried. "And this child, conceived out of wedlock, was your doing as well then. I warrant this has all been some diabolical trickery to ruin me, to drag my family name down into damnation."

"How say you this?"

"Your innocence is a wicked ruse. I see you now! You've lured me to mortal sin, but no more!" Hadley raised his arm, ready to swing. Margharet closed her eyes tight, bracing for an impact that never came.

The hand around her arm weakened suddenly, and as she opened her eyes Hadley collapsed in front of her. Behind him, wielding a small but entirely adequate rock, stood Reverend Allen.

"Get in. Hurry!"

Margharet wailed in shock. Reverend Allen boosted her struggling, weakened body into the wagon as best he could.

As the horses clopped frantically along the dirt road leading out of St. Edmund, Reverend Allen looked back to where the girl lay writhing between boxes and hay. He begged her to muffle her cries, but it was no use.

Margharet's labor had begun.

Chapter 35

Present Day. St. Edmund, Massachusetts.

"Going out to the marker tonight, huh?"

Edgar nodded at the image of Dade on his screen. Just a few hours now stood between Edgar and the answer to the cemetery marker mystery. The snow had finally melted, and he'd just confirmed with Shelby that she'd be able to join him and Corinthian for the night's adventure. He glanced anxiously at his supply bag and the flashlights propped next to the bedroom door. All was ready; there was nothing to do now but wait.

"Any guess as to what you think will happen?"

"My guess? Hidden trap opens under the grass," Dade deadpanned. "You fall in to die a horrible death. Worse, nobody's around when it happens, so you just disappear, never to be seen again. That's how you become a statistic, my friend. Any luck on that book?"

"Wait, are you saying you don't think anything will happen?"

"I'm afraid you mistake my sarcasm for a dismissal of the possibilities," Dade said as he leafed through a magazine off-screen. "Whoever created that cemetery marker didn't want its secret to be easily found. That means anything could happen."

Edgar leaned back in his chair. "Somebody was meant to find it. It's meant to be opened, or removed, or whatever it's going to do when we push those buttons in. Otherwise there'd be no buttons at all, right?"

"*Huh.*" Most of Dade had now moved off-screen. "Guess you'll be finding out soon enough. What about that book?"

"Nothing new, I'm afraid."

"Yeah," Dade sounded dejected. "Look, kid, I've gotta let you go. Happy hunting. Let me know what you find. If I don't hear from you, well –"

Edgar watched as the screen went dark. *Nice.* He felt bad about coming up empty on Dade's book quest, but what could he do? Even if it was actually in St. Edmund, there was a very good chance it was stored away somewhere, maybe even forgotten. It might never show up at all.

If it even exists.

Outside, the sun was slowly moving toward the horizon. Edgar donned his cemetery tour garb, which was only slightly more Victorian than his normal apparel. From the period-inspired black wool jacket and vest to an appropriately foppish white ruffled bow tie, Edgar's outfit was impeccable. A pair of small round spectacles he'd recently found at a local antiques store completed the illusion. Before long he was standing in front of the mirror, looking every bit the 18th century gentleman tour guide.

Now to act the part.

Chapter 36

A cold mist lay across the haphazard rows of gravestones. At the cemetery entrance, three beams of light appeared, winding quickly back toward where the *Ophelia Goodwicke* marker stood.

"Can you believe this?" Shelby grabbed Edgar's shoulder in excitement, making his flashlight beam dance chaotically across the stones.

"My dear, calm yourself," Corinthian chuckled. "Even the tourists don't get this fidgety!"

"But what if we're being watched right now! Aren't you scared? I mean, you know, it's just... all these graves! It really is spooky."

"Ghosts, milady?" Corinthian said. "I'm sure you attract only the most chivalrous and handsome spirits to your side."

Shelby laughed. "That's not very reassuring."

In the distance, another flashlight beam could be seen moving in the night mist.

"Look!" Shelby whispered.

Edgar squinted his eyes at the swinging gait of the flashlight. "That's John Creyle's nightly tour group. Nothing to worry about." Edgar could almost hear John's monotone delivery from across the grounds.

A few more steps and they were face-to-face with their destination. The metal marker glowed greenish-blue in the damp air. The flashlight beams highlighted the beveled metal letters on the surface, cutting sharp, black shadows into the green patina.

"Different than in the daytime, isn't it?" Edgar said.

"It's beautiful," Shelby whispered. "I can see why you enjoy doing the tours."

"My dear friends, I'd love to bask all night in this eloquent, taphophilic glow, but I must remind you both of the time," Corinthian rocked on his heels.

"Right," Edgar said. "Let's do this."

Moving to either side, Edgar and Corinthian pushed in the two pointing hand buttons. The marker shifted slightly as two metal clicks reverberated within. Something had released. Edgar paused, remembering Dade's dire — if sarcastic — warning.

"What is it, lad?" Corinthian said.

No darts. No trap door.

"Nothing."

The metal shell was lighter than Edgar expected as they lifted it away. *Lift thy mortal veil.*

"What do you see, lad?" Corinthian leaned close. "Quick Shelby, bring your flashlight. Is there something there on the base? What is –? Dear me, could that be a book?"

"I don't think so," Edgar's eyes focused on lines of text etched into a strange metal plate.

"It's a plaque," Corinthian whispered. "It's another bloody riddle."

"Zinc oxide, too," Edgar noted. "Same as the marker."

"Can we pry it off the base?" Corinthian's fingers fumbled greedily about the edges but couldn't get a grip. "We can't leave it here for others to see."

"We don't have time," Edgar snapped photos of the plaque. "We're just going to have to put the marker back onto the base when we're done. In the meantime –"

Edgar pulled out a scroll of tracing paper and a stick of charcoal and handed them to Shelby. "– care to do the honors?"

"Me?" Shelby said.

"Nothing better than a good grave rubbing."

Edgar held the paper roll against the plaque. "Just rub the charcoal back and forth across the paper."

Once Shelby finished, the cover was quickly snapped back into place and they gathered their things to leave.

"This is the craziest thing I've ever done in my life!" Shelby said. "I can't believe something has been hidden in there all this time, just waiting to be discovered."

"Like a young girl's heart," Corinthian waxed.

"Oh my God," Edgar mumbled as they hurried out of the cemetery.

Chapter 37

Minutes later they were back at the tavern. Corinthian quickly arranged a refresher for them all — beer for him, soft drinks and curly fries for his companions — as they settled into their booth.

"Another bloody riddle," Corinthian fumed again. Downing his entire pint of dark stout, he templed his fingers in front of his face as he contemplated the unrolled grave rubbing. The beer failed to remove his pained expression.

"Be of good cheer, Corinthian," Shelby soothed in her best attempt at a British accent. "This just means you get to enjoy my company a little longer."

"Please dear, that was a most horrifying sound," he patted her arm. "Pray leave the *mother tongue* to the professionals."

"At least it got a smile," Shelby replied. "So, are these Biblical references or what? This sounds like Judgment Day stuff."

The verses whispered from the charcoal's back-and-forth shading:

When the house of God is
Full man thy weary
Persecuted soul will
Falsely walk the level'd gloom
The lost must come to Church's Gate
Innocent and guilty
Ones alike will to truth

Descend

"That's what I first thought as well," Edgar said. "But these verses have everyone going to Hell — innocent and guilty alike — where the truth apparently will be found. That doesn't sound like the Bible I know. Although now that I think about it, the Puritans held the belief that everyone was damned from the start, so maybe it's referring to that."

"Puritanical," Corinthian repeated quietly as his fingers played along the words. At *Church's Gate* his hand stopped, then pulled back. "No, I'm sure this isn't a traditional scripture reference. I must admit I'm baffled. Barkeep?" He motioned for a refill.

"I know that symbol," Edgar said, tapping the star shape at bottom. "This is a star anise; it appears on Margharet Fullman's and Hadley Williamson's graves, too."

"Star anise," Corinthian said. "Sometimes used for healing. Also does wonders for a bland shepherd's pie. However, here it appears to be nothing more than decorative."

"I'll tell you what's not decorative, though," Edgar said. "Look at how the first word of each line is shifted up."

"Shifted up?" Corinthian focused on where Edgar's finger was pointing. Sure enough, the first word of each verse was slightly higher than the rest. "Dear me. How did I miss that?"

"What's so important about that?" Shelby asked.

"Read only all the shifted words, from top to bottom," Edgar said.

"*When... Full... Persecuted...*"

"No, look, *Full* and *man* are both shifted up. Read them as one word."

"*Full man!*" She looked at Edgar and began to laugh. "Barnes Fullman!"

"Who else? Read it all!"

"*When... Fullman... Persecuted... Falsely... The... Innocent... Ones.* Edgar, that's a sentence. It's a hidden sentence — a secret message!"

"It's more than that," Edgar said. "It's a damning accusation against Barnes Fullman."

"This is unbelievable," Shelby grabbed another curly fry. "It's like being in a movie or something. But I still don't understand. Why would someone destroy all evidence of Fullman's existence, but at the same time put his name in these verses? Why would someone hide the truth and yet preserve it?"

"My dear, it's been done before," Corinthian said. "When Shakespeare helped write *The King James Bible*, for instance, he was so bold as to hide his autograph in the Psalms."

"William Shakespeare helped write the Bible? Corinthian, are you kidding?"

"*The King James Bible*," Corinthian corrected. "Count down 46 words in Psalm 46 and you find the word *shake*. Count 46 words up from the end of the same passage and you find *spear*. Quite clever, really — 46 being the age Shakespeare supposedly was when he helped write it."

"*Though the mountains shake with the swelling*, right?" Edgar reached for a handful of fries. "And, *he breaketh the bow, and cutteth the spear*. Just a coincidence, Corinthian."

"Anyway, whoever did this intended only the right person to find it."

"I guess that's us," Shelby said. "But other than Barnes Fullman doing something bad to the *Innocent Ones* — whoever they are — this doesn't make any sense. What now?"

"There's nothing more to do tonight," Corinthian said. "I suggest we roll up our parchment, keep this little discovery to ourselves, and allow tomorrow to bring fresh revelations."

Chapter 38

Edgar and Shelby strolled along empty cobblestone streets toward her home. What a night it had been!

Shelby's hand soon found Edgar's, and despite his excitement at their discoveries, he found himself even more speechless than usual. He dared a glance, catching her face in exquisite profile as light from a streetlamp danced across her features. He looked away again, embarrassed, but couldn't shake the image of her now frozen like a snapshot in his mind.

"Look at those stars!" Shelby said as they took one of the unlit side streets toward her house. "You know, it takes centuries for even the closest stars' light to reach us. Isn't that crazy? It's like, we don't know if those stars are even there anymore. All this starlight we see is really super old. My dad used to take me skygazing when I was a kid. Look, that bright one is Saturn. Did you know that stars twinkle but planets don't?"

"I've heard that," he said. "Because of the distance starlight is weaker, so it has a harder time getting through the atmosphere. Just think, It travels all that way, but then almost loses it right at the end."

Two hands found Edgar's cheeks. Before he knew it, Shelby's lips were pressed hard against his. He felt her giggling as his hands found her waist, causing him to pull back.

"What? What are you laughing at?"

"Edgar, you speak *stars!*" she beamed, and pulled him back for more.

Chapter 39

An enveloping mlange of mothballs, funerary flowers and ancient pipe tobacco greeted Corinthian as the door to the Cemetery Administration Building swung open. His nose was oblivious to the pungent bombardment; having lived there for many years he'd long ago grown used to its peculiar air. His overcoat, scarf and mittens fell to the floor as he stumbled in. There was no one to notice his lack of etiquette, and he really didn't give a shit.

He caught sight of his reflection in the hallway mirror and chose to ignore the old man staring back at him. His alcohol-induced self-pity would just have to wait.

He was such a fool. He should have guessed. He'd mowed and trimmed countless times around that marker and never suspected. *Ophelia was not dead after all.* He bared teeth at his reflection. She lingered still, and diligently, too — guarding her special secret, while men fought and died around her. His own pathetic sword had been a pair of valiant hedge clippers.

Ridiculous old fool. You almost ran out of time.

Corinthian's hand groped deep into a small shelf in the wall, and was soon rewarded with the feel of smooth, cold metal. Quickly unscrewing the flask lid, he took a deep, burning swig.

The descent to the basement office was a creaky, wooden curve of wooden beams, bringing him down in a tight arc to the bottom, where centuries of musty documents lay piled and forgotten. He switched on the hanging light as he came to the bottom step and brought the unfolded page up to the bulb.

There it was.

That damned finial — the same star anise illustration he'd seen in the grave rubbing. It sat cradled between a colorful assortment of other alchemical symbols and illustrations, but larger than the rest. Corinthian laughed as he took another gulp from the flask. *Star of the show.* Bloody funny, that.

The background shifted slightly on the edges of his field of vision as he slid slowly into the old desk chair. The leathery paper felt warm against his fingers. He fondled it lovingly as he let the image of the star anise spin against the backdrop of the swinging 75-watt bulb.

His mother sure could cook. She'd boil stuff over the stove, throwing in hound's tongue and sage and honey and all sorts of wonderful gifts from nature. *The wisdom is in the living world around us,* she'd smile as he peeked over the rim of the pot, curious as to what smelled so remarkably pungent and alive. Later, when he was old enough, she'd send him out into the fields for various ingredients. And when he'd return she would tell him about a book — a *Grimoire,* she called it — that had a deeper wisdom and power than anything she could conjure.

You will levitate with the wisdom hidden there, my child. And you shall never grow old. And perhaps you shall even find it. I think you shall, dear Corinthian, for it is yours by blood.

It had been so long since he'd tasted her peach cobbler. He took one more stab at the flask, then slammed it to the desk. "Yours," he slurred, swaying in the chair. Like England's Prince Charles, waiting a lifetime to finally — *maybe* — be king for a day. He glanced down at the tantalizing page, his only palpable evidence that the book was anything more than a child's fable.

Mine.

He let his head fall gently to the desktop as the star anise continued to dance. Soon it was replaced by a young maiden, leading him seductively up an ancient staircase cutting through a golden meadow. She turned to him, gesturing with a delicate, porcelain hand, drawing him up toward the promise of a golden sunrise.

Levitate, she whispered seductively. And he did.

Chapter 40

Edgar's cellphone vibrated in his coat pocket. He looked to find a text message waiting for him:

"Tick-tock."

He smiled and texted back to Shelby, only a few classrooms away:

"Tempus Fugit!"

Her response came fast:

"Whatever! C U at lockr!!!"

Corinthian had called Edgar at school earlier that day. He had a possible clue, he said, and he couldn't wait to share it that evening.

Edgar glanced over his shoulder. Luckily, the thugs were occupied, flicking a paper football back and forth. He held the phone discreetly under the table and thumbed his response:

"U want 2 B seen with me? U must B crazy!"

The screen remained silent for several seconds, then came her response:

"Gasp N wonder at my audacity."

Edgar couldn't help but smile. He could still feel her warm lips against his from the night before, could still feel her pull him close. He felt dizzy thinking about it. Packing up his books, Edgar waited for the bell, still five long minutes away.

Shortly after he reached his locker, Shelby approached.

"Omigod, I'm going crazy! What's up with Corinthian?"

"No idea," He paused, struck by Shelby's blue eyes.

"What is it? Do I have something on my face?"

"You're just – really beautiful," he stumbled over the words. He'd never said anything like that to anyone.

"I'm sorry, but I think I need to kiss you again right now," Shelby whispered, leaning in.

Edgar swallowed hard and awkwardly moved toward her. His lips were just about to touch hers when something made him pause. To his right, his eye caught Shelby's two friends, Becky and Amanda, standing across the hall, their books held like shields to their chests.

"Oh my God," Becky said, her mouth gaping. "What nightmare did I wake up in this morning? Shelby, what is this? Are you rehearsing for a play or something? Please tell me you're rehearsing for a play. Because otherwise it looked like you were about to kiss this freak!"

"You're lucky we came along when we did, Shelby," Amanda jumped in nervously. "I don't think you were aware, but you almost had *Ed-Gore* mouth on your face!"

Edgar was about to say something very insulting in response when he felt Shelby's hand squeeze his.

"We've already kissed," Shelby boasted defiantly. "Last night, in fact. I don't know where he learned to kiss like that, but he's pretty amazing. You two don't know what you're missing."

"You wha...?" Amanda teetered. "Shelby, is this some sort of pity-date thing? I mean I've seen that on YouTube, where a beautiful girl goes out with an ugly creep, and they make a video of it and it goes viral, and the girl comes out looking like an angel. Is that what you're doing? Ew, are you making videos of you two kissing?"

"Shelby, God didn't make you the sizzler you are so you'd have to date weirdoes," Becky chided. "You're hot

— you don't have to shop consignment."

"You can both shove it!" Shelby yelled, drawing the attention of everyone in the hall. "I'm tired of living in your conceited shadows. You'll be old and ugly someday, and you won't be able to stand yourselves anymore — because you'll finally look like who you really are. In the meantime," she turned back to Edgar and gave him a long, smoldering kiss, "I've got my sizzler right here."

Chapter 41

Cora and Gertrude sat on a bench a block away from the tavern. Around them, pigeons strutted and fluttered for their bits of feed.

The women glanced up occasionally, keeping an eye on the tavern door. They'd seen Edgar, Shelby and Corinthian enter there a few minutes previous, and had quickly called Stephanie, who'd advised them to hold tight until she got there. Something was up, she said. She could feel it.

"You think the cemetery marker was under his nose the whole time and he didn't know?" Cora spat. "He played me. Played me to get closer to the clue."

"Who on earth are you talking about?" Gertrude said. "Harknell again?"

Cora gazed into the distance and said nothing.

"As I thought," Gertrude said.

"Don't matter," Cora responded quietly.

The two sat in silence for a bit, watching the other side of the street for signs of their quarry.

"She's late," Gertrude checked her watch.

"Said she'd be here, didn't she? But I still don't – " Cora stopped short as her friend's hand touched her arm. From around the corner a few blocks way, a tall, elegantly dressed woman appeared, walking toward them with a runway-model glide.

"They're in there, including your daughter," Gertrude said, jerking her thumb toward the tavern.

"Disappointing. Have you studied the lines of text?" Stephanie said.

Cora and Gertrude had watched in disbelief the night before as Edgar, Shelby and Corinthian lifted the Ophelia Goodwicke marker off its base. The two old women did the same once the trio was gone (they were relieved to find the marker surprisingly light) and promptly emailed photos of the hidden plaque with those puzzling verses to Stephanie.

"Course I have," Gertrude replied.

"So you noticed, then, the hidden message that mentions Fullman?" Stephanie crossed her arms.

Cora pulled out her copy of the verses. "Are you sure?"

Gertrude slapped her hand. "Put that away, fool!"

"*When Fullman Persecuted Falsely The Innocent Ones,*" Stephanie recited smugly. "I'm surprised you both missed it."

"That doesn't even make sense," Gertrude brushed herself off. "This is an idiotic goose chase. I say we sit back and let those three wear themselves out. I'm too old to be wasting my time on childish games."

Stephanie tucked some loose strands of platinum blonde behind an ear. "You will both do what is needed to find that Grimoire."

"*Find it?*" Cora made quick eye contact with Gertrude, who had stopped moving at the mention of the book. "But that's just a silly myth."

"Cards on the table, girls, as there's simply no time left. I know you and Gertrude would love nothing more than to get your hands on that book, as would I. The Grimoire is real. In my opinion these clues confirm it. Now we can either let Harknell get his drunken hands

130

on it — God knows why he even wants it — or we can be the new owners of St. Edmund's greatest lost relic, as well as possess its legendary power."

Cora and Gertrude stared at each other, crestfallen. They hadn't anticipated sharing the book with Stephanie. Unfortunately, she'd just called them both out. There was nothing to do now but play along.

"I think we're in agreement, then," Gertrude said, looking intently at Cora. "Aren't we? We'll all use the book."

"I suppose we are," Cora gritted her teeth. "We'll share." The last word stretched out as a venomous *shaaaaare.*

"And just in time, too." Stephanie's gaze trailed across the street to where Edgar, Shelby and Corinthian were leaving the tavern. "Now why am I not surprised to see which direction they're headed?"

"Himmelhaus," Gertrude whispered as they left their perch and began to follow.

Chapter 42

"My dad used to bring me here to look at the night sky," Shelby squeezed Edgar's hand. "I haven't been here in years. Doesn't look so hot right now, though."

The park commonly referred to as Heaven's Garden normally featured well-trimmed shrubbery, needley conifers and stately oaks. But the recent snowstorm had taken its toll on the manicured hill, leaving a mess of mud and thawing plant roots.

Edgar, Shelby and Corinthian stood at the park gate — a wrought-iron Victorian archway. The afternoon sun cast snaking shadows through the old railing, causing the ground below to appear strangely alive.

Beyond the filigreed entry arch, a series of lonely granite steps ascended to the top of the hill, where nothing stood to meet them.

Corinthian clapped his hands, startling his companions. "My friends, thank you for accompanying me to this most interesting spot. But why are we here, you ask! Simply put, after we went our separate ways last night I was walking home when something suddenly clicked in my head, like a puzzle piece. Edgar, you recall that name I saw on the Historical Society map?"

"How could I forget?" Edgar said. "I couldn't tear you away from that map, but you told me it was nothing. We left empty-handed."

"Then, my lad, allow me to remedy the situation."

Corinthian raised a finger dramatically, then pointed toward their feet. Concealed by dirt and leaves, a word could just barely be seen, etched deep into the bottom stair.

"What is that?" Shelby bent low to brush away some of the covering.

"I don't believe it," Edgar said, as a familiar word became legible.

Himmelhaus.

"You see, I was trying to figure out why that word was spread out on the map, with a letter at every intersection. I'd never seen anything like that on a map before, but it reminded me of tiny breadcrumbs. And then those verses last night –" Corinthian trailed off, rubbing his hand over his grizzled chin. He hadn't shaved in days, nor did it appear that he'd slept much. "You remember the line about *Church's Gate*? We all thought it was referring to an actual gate of a church, yes?"

"What else?" Edgar said.

Corinthian turned his head with impish delight, drawing their attention to a nearby street sign.

"Church Street and Gate Street," Edgar said, his brain churning the words. "This is where Church and Gate intersect. The verses are directions to Heaven's Garden — to Himmelhaus!"

"The name on the map pointed the way to this spot like an arrow," Corinthian grinned. "It was the apostrophe *S* that threw us; it's really an ampersand. But you must look closely; it was intentionally made to look like an apostrophe *S* to fool the less observant."

"So, the lost must come to the intersection of Church Street and Gate Street to find the house of God," Edgar said, looking up the stairs. "To find Himmelhaus. But I still don't understand – there's nothing up there. The stairs just end at the top. Is Himmelhaus the real name of this park? I thought its name was Heaven's Garden. What is this place anyway?"

"Lad, this is where Barnes Fullman persecuted the *Innocent Ones.*"

Chapter 43

April 24, 1724. St. Edmund Island, Massachusetts.

"Hattie!"

Goody Wallace huddled under the darkened window. A growing smell of burnt oak and cedar hung in the night air, and she could hear the sound of distant, frenzied voices trailing down from the hill.

"Hattie!" she called louder into the open window. A small flicker of candlelight warmed the ceiling.

"Bethany!" a voice whispered from inside. "Why come you here now? You must flee!"

"There is no haven for me now," the old woman replied. "But you will make it through this unjust persecution unscathed. I've foreseen it."

"But Goody Hartridge, and Mary Harris..."

"We shall ne'er see our companions again. Nor, I suspect, shall you see me."

"You are fleeing then. Good, I..."

"No, I must stay to create diversion. You were right about the reverend. His love for our dear Margharet has guaranteed her safe transport away from here. I do have one favor to ask of you."

A worried, wrinkled face appeared in the window, pale blue from the cold moonlight. Below her, Hattie Wilde saw Bethany Wallace, as well as a small, familiar object in her outstretched hand.

"Bethany, no. You are the keeper..."

"No longer. The *Ancient Crafts* must live on. You be the only other who knows how to wield it properly — and who is not yet suspect."

"You condemn me!"

"No, you must hide this now. The wisdom in the book will perish forever if it is found with me. Quickly now!"

Goody Wilde pursed her frail lips, then swept the book into the darkness of the cabin. "I risk all, Bethany. Pray you say nothing against me. My daughter's life would be forfeit as well."

The sound of angry voices caught their attention. The villagers were thronging back down the hill, in search of those they'd missed. Goody Wilde rushed to put out the flickering candle.

"The *physicks* are yours now," Goody Wallace clasped her friend's hand through the window. "Yours and your descendants'. I bless you with this gift. Be well."

And then she was gone.

In the dark, Hattie Wilde held the Grimoire close and stayed deathly still. Horrible screams echoed through the trees (one of which was, she was certain, that of her dear friend Bethany Wallace) while she waited and prayed for a graceful, peaceful release for her unfortunate companions.

And just when she thought they might never end, the terrible echoes trailed away and were gone. A soft morning blue peeked in through the windows, slowly lifting the heavy shadows from around her.

For better or worse, both she and the Grimoire had made it safely through the night.

Chapter 44

Present Day. St. Edmund, Massachusetts.

"Corinthian, are you saying something bad happened on this hill?"

"On this delightful, well-manicured vista?" Corinthian wheezed, sarcastic, as they trudged up the hill. "Take it from me, lad, this picturesque plateau surely has a story or two yet to be told."

"Great," Shelby said.

A stunning view of the vast Atlantic horizon greeted them as they reached the top — along with a fresh breath of icy wind.

"Look, there's the lighthouse over in Mayhem," Shelby said, relaxing into Edgar's arms. "You should see it at night from up here."

"Count me in. So who owns this hill anyway?"

"The ladies of the St. Edmund Historical Society oversee this property," Corinthian replied coldly. "As far as I know, the deed has always been in their possession. They do keep it well tended, don't they? Except for now, that is. Let's begin our search for anything unusual. You two start over there and see what the periphery offers."

Edgar and Shelby took to the edges, their eyes glued to the ground.

"So, I guess you like me then," Edgar said, once they were out of earshot.

"Guess so."

"Truth is, I like you, too. I have for a long time, I guess. I tried not to, though. I never thought you'd go for someone like me, someone so out-there. I certainly never imagined you'd do what you did at school today. That took some guts."

"I guess you're just my kind of out-there, Mr. Wilde," she said without taking her eyes off the ground. "Anyway, tomorrow's going to be interesting. Looks like it's time for me to find some new friends."

"Just be yourself. They'll find you."

Shelby gave Edgar a playful bump, throwing him off-balance. "Why Edgar, I believe that's the sweetest thing you've said to me."

"I just mean..."

"I know what you mean," Shelby giggled. "That was quite the romantic compliment. I'll carry that with me in the days to come, along with this –" she grabbed Edgar's hand and swung it triumphantly back and forth.

"Oww!"

She reached for his other hand and began twirling him playfully.

"No, no! We'll be having none of that!" he laughed, pulling his hands to the safety of his coat pockets.

"A waltz, then?" she teased, leaning in to brush her nose against his. "Surely you have some moves tucked away in your musty old Victorian vault. Come on, what did they do back then? A little swing, maybe?"

"*Swing dancing?* Are you kidding?" Edgar hollered, playfully aghast.

"Don't worry, I'll teach you. You'll be great! Got the height for it, too. Hey, look –" She bent down and dug out a piece of old brick. "What's an old brick doing up here?"

Edgar kicked at the scattering of old, blackened bricks, broken bits of granite, and shards of scorched glass embedded in the dirt — all of which he'd been too distracted to notice until now.

"It's all over the place. There must have been a building or something. I suppose that's where those old granite steps originally led to."

"What do you think happened here?" Shelby kicked some of the rubble with her boot.

Edgar bent to the ground, picking through the bits and pieces. "Had to be a fire. A long time ago, too."

"How do you know?"

Edgar held up a mass of primitive, half-melted nails, twisted and locked forever in a tortured embrace. "See this? Whatever was here was constructed with hand-made, wrought-iron nails. Machine nails didn't come along until after 1800 or so."

Chapter 45

The beige spiral cord swung against the kitchen wall as Aubry replaced the phone on the receiver.

According to Felicia, the Historical Society was on the move, following Edgar, Corinthian and that Emerson girl. What was Stephanie thinking, allowing her own daughter to get involved?

Wiping her hands on a towel hanging from the refrigerator door, she stared out the window toward the garden. Had she been too indulgent? Her grandson was entirely capable, but things had certainly gotten serious.

She was especially grateful that Felicia was now one of the four Historical Society committee members. When Aubry nominated her for the vacant position the other three members had put up quite a fight. Felicia was an outsider, but her knowledge of local history and her active role in the community — and Aubry's sponsorship — had finally earned her a reluctant greenlight from the committee. From that moment on, Felicia had been the best fly on the wall Aubry could have hoped for.

She sat in front of the little wooden box on the coffee table.

"All this fuss," she whispered, resting her hand on the box. When she opened her eyes again the light coming through the windows sparkled with renewed energy. Or was it her? She removed her hand and took a deep breath.

It was time for a walk. She loved to stroll on winter days like this, when the sun was crisp yet chilly. *There was a time for every truth, a deep groove reserved for every turn of life.* She thought of Edgar's mother, the years since her passing. Yet her beloved daughter's voice lived on in Aubry's ears, a spirit-memory caught forever in her heart. And smiling at her through Edgar's eyes.

She smiled. There is no winter without a spring to wake it.

Bundling herself in mitts and winter coat, Aubry Wilde opened the door to the cold day and turned toward Heaven's Garden.

Chapter 46

Hearing their approach, Corinthian greeted Edgar and Shelby with a wide grin that in the sunlight took on the color of green tea.

"Any luck?"

"A very old structure once stood on this spot," Edgar said. "Looks like a fire brought it down."

"A big one, too. England probably saw it across the bloody Atlantic. I've been finding the leftovers as well."

"Corinthian, what's that behind you?" Shelby pointed toward an odd, flat piece of metal protruding from the dirt where Corinthian sat. "Oh my god, please don't tell me that's a coffin. I will freak out on you both right now."

Edgar dropped to his knees, scraping away more packed dirt from around the metal. His inner archaeologist had completely taken over. "Seriously, Corinthian, what is this?"

"I dare not imagine," Corinthian stood up and tried working a kink out of his back. "I had spotted a little exposed bit of metal, and the more I've scraped away, the more of it there's been!"

As Edgar dug and scraped, a bizarre sight began to take shape. Before him, rising from the rest of the metal, was a flat metal cross mounted on a small cylinder.

"It's loose," Edgar tested the cross with his hand. "I know it sounds crazy, but it almost feels like –"

"A handle?" Corinthian knelt beside him, reverently brushing the cross clean of dust. "My goodness, look at that."

Shelby backed away slowly. "Okay, I'm asking again: *Coffin?* Because it looks like a coffin. I mean, there's a cross there and everything."

"I don't think so," Edgar said. "Corinthian?"

"I've never seen a coffin the likes of this. Perhaps that bit of zinc oxide will enlighten us," Corinthian's bushy eyebrows bristled as he pointed to a bit of familiar blue-green peaking through some residual dirt.

"There are numbers here," Edgar said incredulously as his fingers scraped away the soil.

1724.

"Dear me," Corinthian whispered. "Our favorite year."

And there was more. Edgar squinted his eyes as long-forgotten words were exposed once more to the light of day. "This looks like Latin. Corinthian – ?"

"*Intrare non poteris regnum Dei beatus. Ad mortem festinamus peccare desistamus.* A delightful little dirge. Basically it says, *You will not be able to enter, blessed, the Kingdom of God. To death we are hastening, let us refrain from sinning.* Certainly sounds like an epitaph, doesn't it?"

"Seriously," Shelby stood. "If this thing can be opened, I don't think it should be. I mean, it feels really wrong. Right? I think there's something bad under here."

"Fortunately, my dear, this is not a democracy," Corinthian abruptly took hold of the cross. "It's time to find out just what..."

"Wait!" Edgar said.

"Yes, lad?" his hand twitched anxiously on the cross. "I sincerely hope you have something of relevance to add.

146

I must admit the suspense is going straight up my arse."

"You said the Latin translates to *You will not be able to enter, blessed, the Kingdom of God,* right?"

Corinthian's hand gripped the cross tighter.

"Don't you see? Turning or pulling this cross might be construed as a blessing, Corinthian. Which, according to the verses, wouldn't be good for anybody. I don't think this is a real handle. I think it's a trick."

Corinthian held the cross for what seemed an eternity, then finally let go. "If you're blessed, you won't enter. And the cross could be the blessing. Bless my arse, then. A trick."

"It's a warning," Shelby exhaled. "Who knows what would have happened if you'd turned that?"

"And you would have never tried," Corinthian shot back. "May I suggest looking for other possible clues. Even a damned imperfection will do. If Edgar's right and the cross is nothing more than a trap, then there's something else we've yet to discover."

As the other two scoured the slab of metal, Edgar watched Corinthian, now hunched over the far end, sweeping the dusty surface with his long, rooty fingers. His friend was acting very peculiar suddenly, and Edgar wasn't sure if it was simple irritation with Shelby's hesitation, or if there was something else going on.

"Here, I found something," Shelby said.

"What, girl?" Corinthian almost pushed her aside as he spidered over.

"It's just a little star."

"Not just a star!" Corinthian said. "A star anise! Like under the Ophelia verses, and on Margharet's and Hadley's tombstones. Clever buggers, this has to be it. Now, everybody off!" His finger brushed over the symbol as he looked up at Edgar and gave a charming wink. "You'll forgive me, won't you?"

147

"Forgive you?" Despite Corinthian's familiar, friendly countenance, something in his voice was making Edgar's skin crawl. Why would Corinthian need forgiveness?

"You're like a son to me, you know," Corinthian continued. "I don't know if I could have gotten this far without you."

"I'm sure you wouldn't have, Mr. Harknell," a female voice responded from behind them.

Chapter 47

Edgar, Shelby and Corinthian spun in surprise. At the top of the stairs stood Stephanie Emerson, flanked by Cora and Gertrude.

"Mom!" Shelby exclaimed. "What are you doing here?"

"You three are faster than I'd expected," Corinthian bowed. "Cora, I certainly misjudged your girth."

"You can stick it where the sun don't shine, Harknell!" Cora shot back.

"This is private property," Stephanie interjected coolly. "The St. Edmund Historical Society owns this property, and you three are clearly trespassing. If you do not leave now, we'll be forced to call the authorities."

"But mom, you'll never believe what we've just –" Shelby started.

"Corinthian Harknell," Stephanie continued, ignoring her daughter. "I'd hate to see your services to our community come to an abrupt end, but let me be clear: I'm not without the means to make your life difficult."

"Sorry to disappoint you, but I've simply come too far to stop now," Corinthian retorted. "Summon your police. You know it will be too late. The book will still be mine."

"Book?" Edgar shoved himself into the fray. "Corinthian, what's going on here?"

"It's a very special book, Edgar," Corinthian's eyes

shone. "Below our feet, it's waiting to be reunited with this –" He pulled out an old, folded page with strange markings. "This sheet belongs to a wondrous book of incantations, lost now for over two centuries."

Stephanie, Cora and Gertrude gasped as one as the page unfolded before them.

"A page from the Grimoire!" Gertrude said in disbelief.

"The legend is true!" Cora swooned.

"And good old Dade Davis down in St. Augustine – he certainly drooled over the finder's fee I offered. You'll give him my regrets, won't you, Edgar? I do appreciate his zeal, and I know for a fact he had the best book scout in all of New England looking for it."

"Me," Edgar said. "I'm Dade's book scout in New England. Corinthian, you used me to find this book. This whole time we've been trying to solve the Fullman mystery, why didn't you just tell me what you were really after?"

"Oh, we've had a rollicking good time, haven't we? I am certainly in your debt. But I couldn't risk you finding it first, could I?" He turned back to the three women, dabbing his forehead with a monogrammed handkerchief. "Couldn't risk these three somehow finding out about it before me, either. I know you ladies do want to see it, though. Care to join us? You can't have the Grimoire, of course, as I know you'd prefer, but you'll be among the select few who witness the restoration to its rightful owner."

Cora strutted forward and pushed a gnarled finger into his chest. "The Grimoire is ours! The Historical Society has always been its rightful guardian."

"Yours? Until recently you thought it nothing but a myth, though ironically it was you three who were sworn to protect it," Corinthian said dismissively. "And now you deem yourself witch-worthy? Why, you didn't even remember this secret door, located right here on your own property. It must be a bitter turn. I think it's time I absolve you of your *raison d'tre* so you can get on with your pathetic lives."

"No!" The three women moved toward him, but it was too late. Corinthian had pushed the star anise button. The door broke free of the earth, rising upward on a spring-loaded hinge. A breath of dank, ancient air exhaled past them. Corinthian refolded his handkerchief and stuffed it in his jacket pocket.

"Manner usually dictates ladies first, but I see none are present. Oh, wait, there's one!"

Before anyone could react, Corinthian had Shelby in a firm lock.

"Corinthian! What are you doing?" Edgar yelled.

"What the *hell?*" Shelby twisted hard to untangle herself from Corinthian's strong grip, without success. "Let me go, you crazy old man! What's wrong with you?"

Edgar's attempt to rush Corinthian was brought short as an arm came to rest across Shelby's neck.

"Edgar, who'd have guessed you had a spine? I hate to be clich, but the girl-in-danger thing always works, doesn't it? Let's sum up: I've got Shelby, and don't do anything stupid. Like that."

"Let her go now!" Edgar clinched long fingers into fists.

Corinthian pressed harder into Shelby's neck, causing her to gag. "There's no need to get so ruffled up. I simply need to claim my property. You may come down as well. Just don't follow too closely, right? You'll get your crumpet back soon enough."

Chapter 48

Light from Corinthian's flashlight woke dormant shadows from the cold, mausoleum-like room, causing strange silhouettes to stretch like fingers across the granite ceiling and walls.

Edgar brushed a cobweb from his face as he raced down the stairs. He could hear sounds of struggling coming from the back, but had to stop as a number of menacing wooden contraptions blocked his way.

"I know what these are," he whispered.

"Edgar!" Shelby screamed.

In the far corner, Corinthian was tightening wide straps on a wooden rack. Bound tight to the contraption was Shelby.

"This is a place of deepest reverence, my friends," He buckled the final belt around Shelby's leg. "You Historical Society people have always known, but you hid it! How could you deny the past? The voices screaming in the fire! *The Innocent Ones!*" Corinthian turned a knobbed wheel, causing timbers to groan and Shelby to scream again.

"Corinthian, are you insane?" Edgar yelled. "You don't need to do this. Let Shelby go!"

"Listen to me, Edgar! There were witches here — real ones! There were practicing, powerful witches here in St. Edmund! This hill, this place — this was the exact location of their coven! And then Barnes Fullman built his mansion, his *Himmelhaus*, on top of their sacred site after he condemned, tortured and killed all those innocents who followed the *Ancient Ways*."

"Witch trials," Edgar's eyes were frozen on Shelby as he tried to keep Corinthian talking. "No one has ever uncovered anything about witches in St. Edmund. I think you need to go about 60 miles north."

"It's because he's one of them," Cora spat. "He's a witch! That's how he knows!"

"Don't tell me you don't want to find the Grimoire yourself, Cora!" Corinthian said. "By the way, dear lady, the preferred term is *warlock*." Another turn of the wheel took Shelby's voice to another octave.

"Either way, you are sadly mistaken," Stephanie soothed, seemingly oblivious to her daughter's misery. "That book's a myth; all you've done is uncover a bit of odd paper and a horrible memory of this town's past."

"But you want it!" Corinthian insisted as he turned the wheel an inch more, ignoring Shelby's shriek. "You want the Grimoire! Don't let them deceive you, Edgar – these three women are evil! They aspire to gifts they cannot hope to wield! Only I can truly command the book."

"I don't care, Corinthian! Let her go!" Edgar inched forward. He'd been in a fight or two before, but never with an adult. He was just about to hurl himself onto Corinthian when a shadow from the stairs filled the whole of the cellar.

"Am I late?"

Chapter 49

Aubry stood at the foot of the stairs, the light from above casting her in a luminescent halo of white.

"Grandma!"

"Aubry," Stephanie nodded coolly. "Surprised to see you here."

"No, you're not," Aubry smiled.

Walking slowly around the chamber, Aubry studied a collection of thumbscrews. "This is passing strange," she finally said as she removed her light cotton mitts. "My word, you don't see these anymore, do you?"

"Grandma – Corinthian's gone crazy! He's got Shelby!"

"Find your Grimoire yet, Mr. Harknell? It must be around here somewhere. No? Oh, dear. But you know how rats love paper."

"The *sacred book* was not devoured by a rat infestation," Corinthian smirked. "But I must ask – how do *you* know about the Grimoire?"

"Both our families go back quite a way in this town, Mr. Harknell. Yours is not the only one with roots." She held his stare until she began to giggle. "Oh my, if only you knew which kind of roots to use in your spells!"

"You think this is funny?" Corinthian snarled.

Aubry crossed to Stephanie, Cora and Gertrude. "Ladies, you've done the Historical Society proud, I must say."

"You did this!" Cora hissed at her. "You trained

that boy, and you sent him to help Harknell find the Grimoire."

"All secrets have their day in the sun," Aubry stepped delicately over Cora's accusation. "While I must admit this is one particular day I'd have been pleased to never see arrive. Ah, well. *Que Será, Será.*"

"There's nothing here!" Corinthian's eyes were finally adjusting to the dark, taking in the entire room for the first time. "No papers – no books at all!"

Aubry clasped her hands in feigned regret. "Now that is a pity. Better luck next time. I'm sure you can still perform some wonderful small enchantments of your own. You *can* do that by now, I imagine, even without the book?" She slid her hands neatly into her mittens.

"I am not powerless, madam," Corinthian replied coldly as he raised his hands toward her. "Do not presume me an amateur."

"Don't touch her!" Edgar lunged between Corinthian and his grandmother.

"Enough, young man." Aubry gracefully stepped aside. "While entirely capable of defending me, your services aren't required at this precise moment." Raising a gloved hand, she blew a kiss toward Corinthian. In an instant he was on the ground in an uncontrollable sobbing fit.

Aubry!" Cora said, running to the crumpled Corinthian. "What did you do?"

"I just don't know what happened there," Aubry replied innocently as she walked over to Shelby. Edgar was already releasing her straps and helping her off the ancient torture device. "Sweet child, are you alright? That must have been a fright. I'm sorry it took so long to get you out of this."

"I'm fine," Shelby rubbed her red, raw wrists and rolled her aching shoulders. She glanced down at her assailant, convulsed now on the floor. "Asshole. See if I come to your funeral."

"Now dear, I'm sure you don't mean that," Aubry said.

"You okay?" Edgar asked, cupping her face in his hands.

Shelby palmed away the last of her tears. "You know, that rack thing really works."

"So I've heard," he said. "But on the bright side – I think you're an inch or two taller now."

"Shut up!" Shelby swatted him on the back.

"Oh, my sweetie!" Stephanie sped over and kissed her awkwardly on both cheeks. "I was so worried! I warned you, didn't I?"

"But what happened?" Edgar stared down at his sobbing friend. "I didn't even touch him. But you, grandma – you blew a kiss at him and down he went."

"It's nothing dear," she tucked her arm into Edgar's elbow. "Let's get out of this vile place, shall we? This nasty mildew does a number on my bronchial tubes."

Chapter 50

Felicia Thompson was deep in a box of newly-acquired books when the little brass bell chimed above the door.

"How did it –" she began, but stopped short as a weeping Corinthian Harknell was escorted in by Edgar, Shelby and Aubry, followed by Stephanie and her elderly entourage. Felicia closed the shipment box and smiled. "*Ahhhh,* I see."

"So, what shall we do with this poor fellow?" Aubry said. "He's been quite consumed about finding some mysterious lost book."

"The Grimoire," Felicia nodded, turning to finish her inventory. Corinthian fell fetal on the carpet, sobbing quietly.

"I don't understand," Edgar said. "What in the world is this Grimoire everyone's talking about? And – witch trials in St. Edmund?"

"Don't forget Corinthian thinking he's a witch," Shelby said, giving the man at her feet the stink-eye as she rubbed her sore wrists. "Sorry, but that's a little freaky, too."

"It started off as such a little thing," Aubry ran a finger over the books stacked on the counter. "A gift from the heavens. Stars overhead begat stars below. The healing flower –"

"You're talking about the star anise," Edgar said. "We've seen that symbol all over the place. Somebody's been using it as some sort of clue –"

Aubry's mouth twitched with acknowledgement as her smiling eyes met Edgar's. "Many years ago a town healer named Bethany Wallace used star anise and other herbs to ease the pain of a tumultuous, illegitimate pregnancy. The girl's father went into a rage when he discovered it. He accused Goody Wallace of witchcraft or some such rubbish, along with his own daughter. A farcical trial ensued," Aubry wrung her hands tightly. "A night of torture and death, up there on that hill. The town lost a dozen good souls that night."

"The pregnant girl was Margharet Fullman, wasn't it?" Edgar said. "It was Barnes Fullman's daughter who was pregnant, wasn't it?"

"Before she was tortured to death, Goody Wallace hustled young Margharet out of town, with the aid of a kind reverend," Aubry continued. "The baby's father — a fellow named Hadley Williamson — was found in the street that very same night. Murdered. But not by the witch-hating mob."

"But Margharet Fullman is buried near Hadley Williamson in our own cemetery," Edgar protested. "Margharet died the same night as Hadley, the same night as the town meeting. She didn't escape. She's right there in the cemetery!"

"No, Margharet fled that night, and she lived out her years far away from St. Edmund Island, as did her daughter. Much later, those who still remembered that night erected those grave markers as a silent tribute. The star anise symbol appears in the clues that led you to Himmelhaus, Edgar, not only because it helped to save poor Margharet's life as well as her child's, but also because it was the symbol of their witch coven."

"Aubry, how can even you possibly know all this?" Stephanie said dismissively.

160

"It took years for the truth of it to make its way back out of the shadows," Felicia nodded. "But when it did, the rest of the town finally came to their senses and realized what a horror Mayor Barnes Fullman really was."

"Aubry, I didn't realize you had a sidekick," Stephanie crossed her arms in irritation. "Now I understand why you fought so hard to get Mrs. Thompson into the Historical Society's inner circle."

"Fullman was a murderer!" Corinthian broke in. "They destroyed all trace of that bastard! And rightly so!"

"Oh my, I'm sorry, dear," Aubry said. Leaning down, she gave his heaving shoulder the slightest of touches. His sobbing ceased instantly.

"Thank you," he breathed heavily, looking up at Aubry in reverence. "I don't know what came over me."

"Corinthian is right," Aubry continued. "They set torches to Himmelhaus, the mansion Fullman built atop the witches' coven, as a final act of revenge. The town vowed to remove all traces of the man. His death a few years after the witch trial is anyone's guess. Some say he was down in his cellar when the town climbed the hill with torches. Perhaps he was found there, clinging to his precious witch trial implements. It had been suggested they sealed it up tight, burying him alive. However, I suppose that's one myth dispelled now that we've seen the cellar for ourselves."

"No corpses," Shelby nodded. "I was very clear about that."

"Margharet Fullman was my great-great-grandmother," Corinthian whispered. "Her blood is mine – the Grimoire should be mine."

"If there was indeed a Grimoire, it was surely passed long ago, passed through a window in the dark," Aubry closed her eyes. "I'm sorry for your family's long, silent journey through time, so far away from home, but the book would have traveled far by now, and perhaps found a new family. Give me your parchment of grief now, and let it go."

Taking his hand in hers for the briefest of moments, she leaned in and whispered something to him that visibly lifted Corinthian's shoulders. He stole a shy glance at Edgar and nodded congenially, as if in apology.

"There now, all is restored." She placed her hands in her coat pockets. "Mr. Harknell has been in quite the emotional quandary for some time now, burdened with unnecessary guilt and no small amount of ambition. But I think you'll find him a better person after today. I certainly hope so."

"I have a question," Edgar said. "The founders of the Historical Society went to such trouble to eradicate all traces of Barnes Fullman. But there were so many clues leading to Himmelhaus. It's obvious somebody wanted the truth to be revealed someday. Right?"

"It's hard to shine a light into all corners of the dark," Aubry said lightly. "Who knows why things are as they are? But all is well. Ladies, I think we're in agreement that the best thing to do is re-seal the door, cover it up, and pretend today never happened?"

"For the best," Cora nodded.

"Agreed," Gertrude said.

"We were sworn to protect whatever was up there," Stephanie said. "We'll continue to do so."

"And the book? The lost Grimoire?" Edgar said. "Was it real?"

Aubry paused at the door, glancing up at the little brass welcome bell. "*Que Será, Será.* Edgar. Oh, dear, does anyone have the time? I'm famished."

"Your grandmother is quite the puzzle," Shelby leaned in as they followed her out into the chill air.

"A dream within a dream," Edgar smiled.

Chapter 51

The delicate, white cotton curtains billowed in the cold breeze, like ghosts.

The windows were open wide, and Aubry sat at the kitchen table, her eyes transfixed on the small, wooden box open in front of her. She hadn't seen the inside of the box for many years, but the smell of it — undercurrents of cedar and pine, and a lingering whisper of licorice — were achingly familiar.

There was also, of course, the Grimoire.

The book was awake now, out of the box and opened to a page full of delicate script. The words moved like a waltz across the sheet of yellowed vellum, whispering a past long forgotten. Aubry ran a finger gently along an ancient tear where a page had been torn out. Unfolding the worn piece of parchment taken from Corinthian, she eased it to its rightful place and closed the book tight. A charged, tingling current of electricity pulsed through her.

Together again.

The town of St. Edmund might never have so successfully forgotten the name Barnes Fullman without the diligence of Aubry's own grandmother, Sarah Wilde. But Sarah had left a path for anyone wishing to remember and honor those who had innocently perished that night. Like the book, handed down from Sarah to the young Aubry, the path had been a secret gift.

"What delightful clues you left us, *Mawma*," Aubry whispered to her grandmother's curtains. "Thank you for your gift."

She pulled the book tight to her chest. Her hands looked like fragile glass sculptures against the dark, leather cover. It was time. The book needed a new guardian. And there was only one person in the whole world she could imagine taking on that responsibility.

For every winter, a spring.

Aubry gazed out the open window, waiting patiently for her grandson to arrive home from school.

THE END

EPILOGUE

July 11, 1887. St. Edmund Island, Massachusetts.

Sarah Wilde took a deep breath and then did the unthinkable. She tore a page out of grandmother's most cherished heirloom — a small book of spells that had been in their family for ages.

She'd never have imagined that this would be her task. A wave of nausea clutched at her stomach; she could still feel the rip reverberating inside her. But she could think of no better way to carry out the important task before her.

The vote had been overwhelming. A group would be formed from the St. Edmund community, charged with ridding itself of the taint of its past. Remnants of the infamous Barnes Fullman would be eradicated. His mansion would be burned to the ground. Records would be altered.

The town would forget.

Sarah systematically sorted through the town's century-old historical documents, eliminating any mention of the mayor, or his witch hunt. She sat now in the cemetery administration building office, torn page in hand. There was nothing to do but continue.

Her task was twofold: *Help the town forget. Help her family remember.* Sarah remembered her mother talking about her own grandmother, Hattie Wilde, who was given the book on the very night of the witch hunt in

1724 by a woman named Bethany Wallace.

In the cemetery ledger, she turned to the page documenting the mayor's date of death, scraping it away with a small knife.

Forget.

She dipped the quill pen into the ink and began to write. Though impossible to replicate exactly, her writing was similar enough to the names above and below to pass a casual glance. She also made certain the new, fictional deceased person — Ophelia Goodwicke — had her own special marker in the cemetery, right on top of Fullman's.

Remember.

Someday, she hoped, one of her descendants might figure out the puzzle of Ophelia the Good Witch.

Now it only remained for her to pass on the book. Sarah noted that Aubry, her precocious granddaughter, showed great aptitude. Aubry would almost certainly be the keeper of the Grimoire one day. But she dared not tell her everything.

Sarah blew on the fresh ink and waited for it to dry. She then folded the torn page from the Grimoire and concealed it in the ledger.

"When your secrets are ready to be known, find your way back," she whispered to the folded page. "Your family will be there, waiting for you."

Closing the altered death ledger, she then slid it back into its space on the old, wooden shelf.

And all was forgotten for a while.

www.ingramcontent.com/pod-product-compliance
Lightning Source LLC
Chambersburg PA
CBHW020441180626
46812CB00003B/1344